THE
GREEN
MILE

THE SCREENPLAY

Screenplay by Frank Darabont
Introduction by Stephen King

SCRIBNER PAPERBACK FICTION
PUBLISHED BY SIMON & SCHUSTER
NEW YORK LONDON SYDNEY SINGAPORE

SCRIBNER PAPERBACK FICTION
Simon & Schuster Inc.
Rockefeller Center
1230 Avenue of the Americas
New York, NY 10020

SCRIBNER PAPERBACK FICTION and design are trademarks of
Macmillan Library Reference USA, Inc., used under license
by Simon & Schuster, the publisher of this work.

DESIGNED BY ERICH HOBBING

Manufactured in the United States of America

1   3   5   7   9   10   8   6   4   2

Library of Congress Cataloging-in-Publication Data is available.

ISBN 0-684-87006-1

For Jeff and Jan Kaufman,
who humble me with their courage.

All author's proceeds from the sale of this book
will be donated to ALS research and charities
in the fight against Lou Gehrig's disease.

May there soon be a cure.

CONTENTS

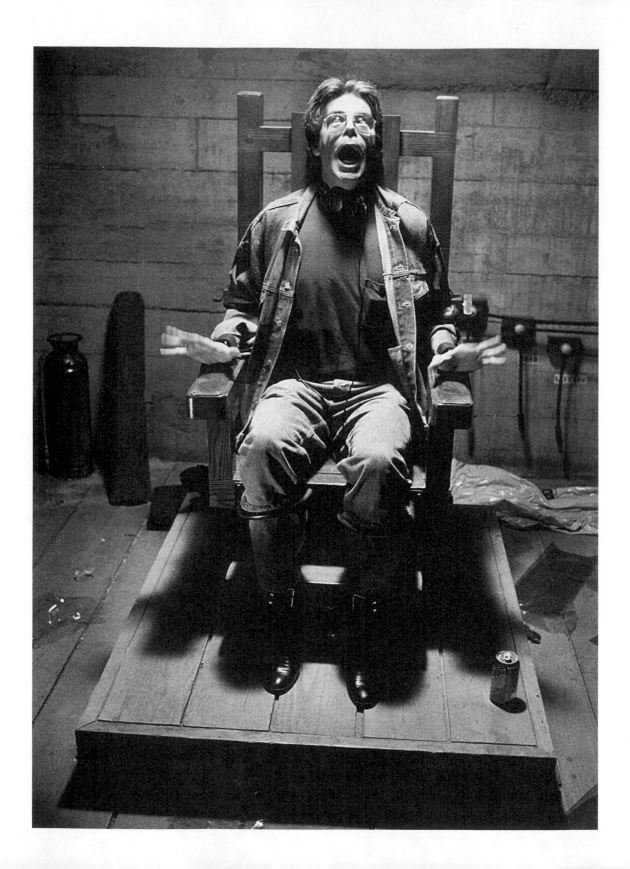

INTRODUCTION

BY STEPHEN KING

Frank Darabont and I have been friends for a long time—ever since he made a short film out of my story "The Woman in the Room." That story's in *Night Shift,* my first collection of short stories, and you might be able to find Frank's film on video, if you're lucky and hit the right deep-pockets video rental emporium (it's worth the hunt). My practice, when students get in touch and ask to make short films out of my stories, has usually been to grant them film rights for a dollar, as long as they promise to send me a copy of the result on videotape and not to exhibit the film for profit without my permission. The so-called dollar deal (Arthur Greene, my accountant and business manager, hates it with a vengeance) has resulted in about twenty films, ranging from the pretty bad to the fairly good. Only two have ever ranked beyond fairly good, in my estimation. One was a horrible-hilarious version of "The Sun Dog" done in Gumby-style Claymation (it's a little bit like those *Celebrity Deathmatch* video shorts on MTV), and the other was Frank's beautiful and moving version of "The Woman in the Room," which is about a son who kills his mother before the cancer infesting her body can eat her alive. Frank's short won an award, and he sent me a copy of the citation. Nice guy.

When he later asked if he could write a screenplay based on my novella *Rita Hayworth and Shawshank Redemption,* I told him to go right ahead, be my guest. I then promptly forgot all about it. Some time later, the script thumped down on my desk, and boy, it was a beaut. The good news? It was as moving as "The Woman in the Room." The bad? It was 'bout forty times as long. I gave Frank permission to show the script around—he could shop it until he dropped, as far as I was concerned—but only in my wildest dreams did I expect it would be made. It was too long, too faithful to the source story . . . and a little too kind. Not even in those wild dreams did I expect it would end up being the screen adaptation of my work that people say they like the best—no mean accomplishment, considering there have been over thirty of them. Even more remarkable is the fact that *The Shawshank Redemption,* clunky title

ix

notwithstanding, has begun to show up near the top of many filmgoers' lists of their favorite movies of all time.

The novella wasn't typical of the rest of my work (many of the people who like the film still don't know it has anything to *do* with my work), and if you'd asked me, after it was done, if I would ever write another story set in prison, I would have asked if you were kidding or running a fever or what. But you never know where the road is going to take you, I guess. In the early nineties I got an idea for an old-fashioned death-row story called *The Green Mile,* and set to work on it after Ralph Vicinanza, my foreign rights agent, asked me if I had any interest in doing a multipart novel *à la* Charles Dickens. I *did* have an interest in trying something like that, which is how I found myself back in prison once more. I guess, like many people who leave Da Joint with good intentions only to find themselves back in stir again, you could say I fell in with bad companions. At least this time there was a creepy element of the supernatural in my story; that made me feel a little more at home.

The Green Mile was originally published in six paperback installments. Frank Darabont called me one night about six weeks before Part One was due to be published (I was at that time deep into Part Three and had only the vaguest idea where I was heading with the story). Frank's call was purely social, a "Hey, howya doin'" kind of thing. We chatted about people we knew, movies we'd seen, what he was up to, and what I was up to.

"Oh," I said, "probably getting ready to make the biggest mistake of my life, that's what I'm up to." And then I told him about my experiment in serial fiction, along with a thumbnail of what the story was about.

There was a long pause when I finished my synopsis. I was about to ask Frank if he was still there when he said in a low and thoughtful voice, "Tell you what, pal— when you get ready to dress that one up and take him around, take him to my house first, wouldja?"

I told him he could have *The Green Mile* right there and then, if he was serious— we could do a handshake deal over the phone . . . but was he really sure he wanted to go back to prison? Hadn't he talked about wanting to do a comedy next, something screwball? Or was that just my imagination?

"Well," he said, "*you* went back, didn't you?"

I agreed that I had. The cellblock wasn't my favorite environment by a longshot, but I *had* gone back. I had to, because I loved the story of John Coffey. And I loved the *mystery* of John Coffey.

"Yeah, that's it," Frank said when I expressed some of this. "Anyway, it sounds like a hell of a good story. Send me the first installment when you can."

So I did. And, as with *Shawshank,* I thought nothing would come of it until something did. What came of it this time was a sprawling and emotionally generous film that most admirers of *The Shawshank Redemption* will likely welcome with open arms. What amazes me isn't how good it is—Frank is, above all, a wonderful and painstaking filmmaker—but how easily and clearly he saw that it *could* be good. I also admire his courage in going back to the same sort of environment—prison—and creating a kind of fraternal twin to his previous picture. I have heard Frank tell the press, "I have the world's smallest specialty—I only make Stephen King prison movies set in the thirties and forties."

Yes . . . and no.

What Frank has actually done is to film two stories I felt with especial keenness, stories which examine (or try to) what happens to the human spirit when the body is imprisoned . . . and perhaps ultimately put to death. Both are grim tales filled with violence, but also filled (I hope) with something better: call it faith and belief. They are stories of goodness in a gray and often hideous world. Frank has caught the goodness as clearly as he has the violence. For that I love and respect him. He's a decent man and a prodigiously talented movie guy.

In a decade where too many movies are cold and glossy and have all the emotional gradient of a customized muscle-car, Frank makes openhearted audience-pleasers that beg us to go with the belly laughs and turn on the old waterworks . . . to *respond,* in other words. He was aided in this by Morgan Freeman and Tim Robbins in his last film; with *The Green Mile* he has put together an even stronger cast, led by Tom Hanks. The result is the sort of film they supposedly don't make anymore, and some of the magic is in the script which follows.

I don't know how Frank feels about it, but as for myself . . . man, I'm delighted to be a repeat offender.

August 28, 1999
Bangor, Maine

INTRODUCTION

BY FRANK DARABONT

I got sent back to prison, and it's Stephen King's fault. There I was, making an innocent phone call just to see how he was doing, and five minutes into the conversation he hit me with the premise of a story he was noodling around with called *The Green Mile.* It really didn't amount to much more than a sketchy description—something about a death-row guard during the Depression and a huge, retarded black inmate condemned to death for killing two little white girls, but who turns out to have magical (even Christlike) healing powers.

Compelling? You could say that. Before we hung up, I asked him to give me first crack at the screen rights if and when he ever finished it. This he promised to do.

Mind you, I never *intended* to go back to prison. Many well-meaning people even advised against it, certain that I would forever pigeonhole myself as a director. These were not unfounded concerns, to be sure. But the truth is, in the five years following *Shawshank,* I'd been offered a lot of directing opportunities that did nothing to motivate my lazy ass back into the director's chair. I find the gig too hard to do it lightly, or just for the dough. Me, I've got to fall in love, and I mean head over heels, to want to direct a movie.

The saga of Paul Edgecombe and John Coffey proved to be love at first sight. Steve's publisher sent me volume one, *The Two Dead Girls,* about a week before it hit the stores. I read it and decided right then and there I had to make the movie—*without,* I might add, the benefit of reading the remaining five volumes or really knowing how the story would turn out beyond the brief phone description Steve had given me a few months before. What I did know was that I was in the hands of a master storyteller, that I was spellbound, that this was King firing on all pistons. In other words, I decided to proceed purely on a leap of faith, convinced Steve would not let me down.

I didn't even bother calling him, that's how excited I was after reading that first volume. Instead, I booked a flight to Colorado, where I knew he was executive producing the miniseries version of *The Shining,* directed by my pal Mick Garris. I wasn't about to let *The Green Mile* slip through my fingers. I was going to find Steve, remind him of his promise to grant me the screen rights, and—if necessary—shake him by the lapels until he hollered uncle.

I flew to Colorado, rented a car, and drove up a mountain. A *big* mountain. During the drive, I had the surreal experience of reliving Jack Torrance's trek up to the Overlook Hotel, a trip perfectly climaxed by my first glimpse of the real-life Stanley Hotel. For those who may not know, the Stanley inspired Steve to cook up the fictional events of *The Shining* during a stay there with his family many years ago. By the time I came up the mountain, the Stanley was repaying its karmic debt to Steve full circle by serving as the filming location for the miniseries. And quite a location it was—gothic and lovely and huge, right out of the pages of his novel.

The Jack Torrance pilgrimage I was undertaking was a full-circle journey for *me* as well. It was reading *The Shining* in high school that started me on my love of all things King, that set me on the path that eventually led to *Shawshank* and *The Green Mile.*

I went inside and found the place crawling with ghosts assembling for a New Year's Eve celebration circa the 1940s, a dazzling array of pomaded fellas and bejeweled dames dressed to the nines in period attire. I was delighted to find among them some good friends who'd shown up from L.A. for the occasion, writers Dave Schow and Christa Faust (Christa's a babe in those period getups, especially since she insists the lingerie be accurate as well). Venturing farther, I entered the ballroom and discovered the man himself, Steve King, lustily conducting a ghostly big band orchestra of jazz-era musicians performing a rip-roaring swing tune. He was dressed in a blinding white tux and having the time of his life, waving his baton and shaking his heinie like Cab Calloway. Mick Garris was directing Steve in the scene and having the time of *his* life as well, judging from the smile on his face.

In between takes, Steve saw me, blinked, and came over to ask what I was doing there. I grabbed him by the lapels, ready to start shaking, and said, "I've come for *The Green Mile.*"

Steve shrugged and replied, "Oh, okay, sure. Hey, you wanna be an extra in this scene?"

And thus were the movie rights to *The Green Mile* acquired. All I had to do was shave my beard off, put on a period tux, and join Dave and Christa as one of Mick's army of undead party revelers. Later on, I also got to help the effects guys pump pus-like goo through plastic tubes concealed in the back of Stephen King's head, which caused a big section of his face to fall *splat!* to the floor in a big, wet, slimy chunk.

Sometimes life just doesn't get any better.

Cut to the present. As I write this, my film of Steve's remarkable story is finally completed and ready to be screened tomorrow night for the very first time before a test audience. I didn't know how much trouble he was getting me into that day he first told me on the phone about this weird little death-row tale he was tinkering with—that I'd wind up going back to prison and spending two years at hard labor before all was said and done. All I knew then was that it sounded like a helluva yarn. I'm glad to say looking back on it now that I was right.

So that's how it happened, ladies and gentlemen of the jury. Big Steve, Patron Saint of Filmmakers, came galloping to my rescue with a great story tucked under his arm. For me, a director experiencing a self-imposed career lull, *The Green Mile* came along like a beautiful woman after a long romantic drought. So what if she bore the blemish of being another prison movie prominently on her face? I fell in love, I tell you, blemish and all. Is a man supposed to ignore true love over a minor imperfection? Don't be silly.

For this blessing, among many others, I owe Stephen King a great debt of thanks. The impact he's had on my life—with his work, generosity, and friendship—can truly never be measured. And I know I speak for all of us, friends and fans alike, when I say how grateful I am to the universe, sheer dumb luck, or whatever higher power may be responsible that he escaped alive (and fundamentally undamaged) from his recent roadside accident. It would have been way, *way* too soon to lose him.

Finally, Steve, on a personal note. Recidivism is an ugly thing. Now that we've earned our parole again, what say we stay out of the slam next time . . .

. . . unless of course you have, like, a really cool World War II POW story in you? *The Shining* meets *The Great Escape,* something like that?

We'll talk.

August 30, 1999
Los Angeles

"THE GREEN MILE"

screenplay by
Frank Darabont

from the serial novel by
Stephen King

Final Shooting Draft

We each owe a death, there are no exceptions...

EXT - FIELD - DAY - 1935 (SLOW MOTION)

Cattails sway in the sepia-toned heat. A small scrap of fabric is snagged in the nettles, fluttering...

Suddenly, a MAN WITH A SHOTGUN comes through the cattails, wiping frame and exiting...

...then ANOTHER MAN...and ANOTHER...armed with rifles, plowing through the brush, exiting frame...

...and now comes KLAUS DETTERICK, a farmer one step above shirttail-poor, a double-barrel shotgun in the crook of his arm. He pauses, horrified, seeing the scrap of cloth. He pulls it loose, turns back, screaming something in anguish...

...and still _more_ men come crashing into view, flooding by us with dreamlike, slow-motion grace. Under it, we hear a sibilant, frightening whisper:

                    WHISPERING VOICE (V.O.)
          You love your sister? You make any
          noise, know what happens?

And off that horrible voice, we

                                        CUT TO:

EXTREME CLOSEUP: EYES

They open, disoriented upon waking, disturbed by the dream. An old man's eyes, confused. Where am I? Is this the past?

Suddenly, a CLOCK RADIO clicks on and pulls us into the present with a prediction of rain. PAUL EDGECOMB, early 80's, realizes where he is and wakes to another day...

INT - PAUL'S BATHROOM - MORNING (PRESENT DAY)

Paul stands at his bathroom mirror, splashing his face, still a bit shaky. The dream clings like a cobweb.

He peers at his reflection. Still here. Still alive. He picks up a hairbrush, starts tidying his hair...

INT - GEORGIA PINES NURSING HOME - CORRIDOR - MORNING

THE OLD AND INFIRM haunt these corridors like ghosts. A WOMAN inches along on a walker. A MAN shuffles by with a rolling I.V. stand. The floor is a limey, institutional green.

Paul comes into view, spry for his age, murmurs an occasional greeting.

THE GREEN MILE

3

(CONTINUED)

INT - BREAKFAST ROOM - MORNING

DOZENS OF RETIREES are having breakfast, sipping weak coffee or tea. Some chat and gossip, some are content to keep their own company, some just stare slackly into space.

Paul enters and sees ELAINE CONNELLY sitting with a few other ladies, sipping tea. She's 80, refined and elegant, his best friend here. She gives him a good-morning smile. He gives her a rakish wink in return, which makes her smile all the more.

Bouyed by the exchange, Paul turns to the serving counter where HECTOR, an orderly, tends the morning shift.

> HECTOR
> Morning, Mr. Edgecomb. Some danish
> for you this morning?

> PAUL
> Just two pieces of dry toast,
> Hector, thanks. Leftover's fine.

> HECTOR
> Dry and cold, same as always. You
> wait a minute, I'll make some
> fresh and hot...

> PAUL
> Cold is better.

The orderly smiles, reaches for the leftover toast.

> HECTOR
> 'Specially on those long walks, am
> I right?

Paul smiles, admitting nothing, waiting as Hector folds the toast into a paper napkin.

> HECTOR
> Don't let Nurse Godzilla catch
> you. She'll raise holy hell. You
> know we're not supposed to let you
> wander off.

He starts to hand the toast over...but pauses instead, peering at him. Perhaps reconsidering.

> HECTOR
> Where do you go every day, huh?
> What do you do up in those hills?

> PAUL
> Just walk. I like to walk.

(CONTINUED)

> HECTOR
> Yeah, well. I still ought not let
> you go...
> > (beat)
> Try not to fall and bust a hip? I
> don't wanna be in no damn search
> party.

He lets Paul have the toast. Paul nods, relieved. He tosses Elaine another look -- catch ya later -- and exits.

INT - HALLWAY PAST KITCHEN - MORNING

Paul slips to the back door unnoticed. Identical red plastic rain ponchos line the wall on pegs. He helps himself to one and eases outside, making good his escape.

EXT - NURSING HOME - ESTABLISHING - MORNING

Nestled in a valley of wooded hills, a drizzly mist rolling over the treetops.

Paul appears f.g., coming up the ridge in his borrowed poncho. He looks back at the valley below, inhales deeply -- this is a man who loves his walks. He pulls a piece of toast from his pocket and starts to nibble as he presses on up the ridge...

EXT - WOODS - MORNING

CAMERA BOOMS DOWN through the trees to find Paul wandering a wooded path, munching a bit of toast, looking for all the world like Red Riding Hood in his plastic poncho.

It's silent here, like a church. The only sounds we hear are the twittering of birds and the hammering of a woodpecker.

WE PAN WITH HIM to reveal an old wooden storage shack along the path up ahead.

INT - SHACK - MORNING

Dark in here, cobwebby and decrepit. We see Paul approaching outside the grimy window. He steps up to the glass and shades his eyes, peering curiously in as we

DISSOLVE TO:

INT - TV ROOM - DAY

Jerry Springer's on the tube, whipping his studio audience into a frenzy. PAN OFF TO REVEAL DOZENS OF OLD FOLKS watching on couches and folding chairs. An old black fellow named MIKE is grousing to a GROUP OF ELDERLY LADIES...

THE GREEN MILE

5

(CONTINUED)

                         MIKE
        Why we always watch this stuff?

                    ELDERLY LADY #1
        It's interesting.

                         MIKE
        Interesting? Bunch'a inbred
        trailer trash, all they ever talk
        about is fucking...

    ...and WE FIND Paul and Elaine sitting together. He seems
exhausted and preoccupied.

                        ELAINE
        Are you all right?

                         PAUL
        Hmm?

                        ELAINE
        You look tired today. You're not
        yourself.

                         PAUL
        I'm fine, I promise.

                        ELAINE
        You're wearing yourself out with
        those walks every day, that's what
        I think. Not that you asked me.

                         PAUL
        I just didn't sleep well, is all.
                    (off her look)
        A few bad dreams. It happens. I'll
        be fine.

MIKE

is at the TV, switching channels past vapid infomercials and
bad daytime TV. He comes upon a Movie Classics channel, which
is playing an old black and white musical -- "Top Hat," with
Fred Astaire and Ginger Rogers. A delighted reaction:

                    ELDERLY LADY #2
        Oh! This is wonderful...

                         MIKE
        Now this here's worth a look...

PAUL

idly shifts his gaze to the TV...and his expression goes slack
with recognition and dismay. Elaine sees the look in his eyes.

THE
GREEN
MILE

                                           (CONTINUED)

He glances away...even briefly considers walking out...but in the end, he can't help himself. The past just caught up with him with a freight-train wallop, and, for once, he decides to ride the rails...

He looks back at the TV. On screen, Fred and Ginger have begun their famous "Cheek to Cheek" number, with Astaire singing in that sublime, easy-go-lucky way of his:

> FRED ASTAIRE
> *Heaven, I'm in heaven, and my heart*
> *beats so that I can hardly speak...*

SLOW PUSH IN on Paul, watching. He'd like to take his eyes off the screen, but the movie has him in a tight grip. Elaine is watching him with puzzled concern:

> ELAINE
> Paul? What is it?

No response. All he can hear is that music, all he can see are those dancers. The figures on TV are gliding with ghostlike grace in their silvery, phosphor-dot world of long ago...

Paul abruptly bursts into tears.

The room goes quiet, everything comes to a standstill. All eyes turn, some concerned, others merely curious. Paul just sits sobbing into his hands, shoulders heaving.

> ELAINE
> Paul...my God...

> PAUL
> It's okay...I'll be okay...

Elaine helps Paul to his feet and leads him out as we

> CUT TO:

INT - SUN ROOM - DAY

Paul is staring out the windows, pensive and drained. It's raining now, pattering the glass and the lawn beyond. Elaine waits across from him, wishing he would speak. Softly:

> PAUL
> I guess sometimes the past just
> catches up with you, whether you
> want it to or not. It's silly.

> ELAINE
> Was it the film? It was, wasn't
> it?

THE
GREEN
MILE

(CONTINUED)

> PAUL
> I haven't spoken of these things
> in a long time, Ellie. Over sixty
> years.

She reaches out, gently takes his hand.

> ELAINE
> Paul. I'm your friend.

> PAUL
> Yes. Yes you are.

Paul wonders if he's even up to talking about it after all
this time...and decides that perhaps he is:

> PAUL
> I ever tell you I was a prison
> guard during the Depression?

> ELAINE
> You've mentioned it.

> PAUL
> Did I mention I was in charge of
> death row? That I supervised all
> the executions?

This _does_ come as a surprise. She shakes her head.

> PAUL
> They usually call death row the
> Last Mile, but we called ours the
> Green Mile, because the floor was
> the color of faded limes. We had
> the electric chair then. Old
> Sparky, we called it.
> (beat)
> I've lived a lot of years, Ellie,
> but 1935 takes the prize. That was
> the year I had the worst urinary
> infection of my life. That was
> also the year of John Coffey, and
> the two dead girls...

> FADE TO BLACK

IN BLACKNESS, A TITLE CARD APPEARS:

> **THE TWO DEAD GIRLS**

> CUT TO:

EXT - GEORGIA COUNTRYSIDE - DAY (1935)

HUNDREDS OF PRISONERS work the fields, pickaxes rising and falling in waves, a prison song being sung in cadence with the work. GUARDS patrol on horseback, rifles aimed at the sky.

A late 20's Ford PRISON TRUCK comes chugging into view along the road, kicking up a long trail of dust in the heat. It seems to be riding unusually low on its rear suspension.

EXT - COLD MOUNTAIN PENITENTIARY - ESTABLISHING - DAY

A Depression-era prison in the south. The prison truck sways down the rutted dirt road toward the main gate...

INT - E BLOCK TOILET - DAY

...while PAUL EDGECOMB, early 40's, stands in a cramped toilet in his guard's uniform, trying to piss. His face is pained, his forehead beaded with sweat.

INT - E BLOCK (THE GREEN MILE) - DAY

BRUTUS HOWELL (nicknamed "Brutal" for his intimidating size, but he's actually rather thoughtful by nature) stands at the entry door of the cellblock, peering out through a viewing slot. He sees the prison truck arrive at the main gate.

He turns and nods to fellow guard DEAN STANTON at the duty desk, then crosses the Green Mile -- a wide corridor of faded green linoleum running some sixty paces top to bottom, with four large cells to a side.

Brutal steps to the bathroom, listens a moment, knocks softly.

> BRUTAL
> Paul? Prisoner.

> PAUL (O.S.)
> Christ. Gimme a minute.

Brutal waits patiently, a bit embarrassed. He finally hears a THIN TRICKLE, accompanied by a stifled groan of pain.

> BRUTAL
> You all right in there?

> PAUL (O.S.)
> For a man pissing razor blades.

The door opens, revealing Paul's pale and sweaty face.

> BRUTAL
> You should'a took the day off,
> gone to see the doctor.

THE
GREEN
MILE

9

(CONTINUED)

                    PAUL
          With a new arrival? You know
          better. Besides, it's not as bad as
          it was. I think it's clearing up.

They hear the truck HONKING as it rumbles up outside. Paul
gives them a nod to resume their positions. Paul walks down
the Mile, passing the cells where the two current inmates
reside -- the first is ARLEN BITTERBUCK, a Washita Cherokee;
the second is EDUARD DELACROIX ("DEL"), a wiry Cajun.

                    BITTERBUCK
          New boy coming in, boss?

                    PAUL
          Never you mind, Arlen, you just
          keep your nose quietly on your
          business. Goes for you too, Del.

Paul arrives at the end of the Mile, takes up a position at an
empty cell. (Down at this end, past the cells, is E Block's
version of the "hole" -- a padded room where violent inmates
are sent to cool off. It isn't used very often...in fact, at
the moment, it's doubling as storage space.)

BRUTAL

peers out the viewing slot as the truck stops outside.

                    BRUTAL
          Damn, they're riding on the axle.
          What'd they do, bust the springs?

He watches GUARDS PERCY WETMORE AND HARRY TERWILLIGER OF E
BLOCK emerge from the truck and step down, turn back...

TIGHTER ANGLE ON BACK OF TRUCK

We get our first glimpse of the new inmate as a pair of
GIGANTIC BLACK FEET step down into the yard...and the rear of
the truck bounces back up on its springs where it belongs.

BRUTAL

sees what's coming, eyes widening slightly.

                    BRUTAL
          Paul? You might wanna reconsider
          getting in the cell with this guy.

                    PAUL
          Why's that?

                    BRUTAL
          He's enormous.

THE GREEN MILE
10

                                        (CONTINUED)

                              PAUL
                    Can't be bigger than you.

Brutal tosses him a look -- just wait. He swings the door open
in a hot flood of daylight, giving us our first good look at:

JOHN COFFEY

is a <u>huge</u> black man, nearly 7 feet tall and 300 pounds, his
massive head shiny and bald, his skin a tapestry of old scars,
his prison overalls (the biggest size they had) ending at mid-
calf. He looks dull and confused, as if wondering where he is
and how he got there. Percy and Harry lead him toward E Block
in shackles. Percy's got his hickory baton out of its custom-
made holster, hollering:

                              PERCY
                    Dead man walking! Dead man walking
                    here!

INSIDE THE CELLBLOCK

Paul can't see them approach from where he stands, but he
can certainly hear Percy:

                              PAUL
                    Jeezus, pleeze-us, what the hell's
                    he yelling about?

Up by the door, Brutal just rolls his eyes. Percy is the first
one through the door, still hollering...

                              PERCY
                    Dead man walking!

...then Coffey enters, ducking low to get through, his shadow
blotting out Brutal and Dean as his massive frame fills the
door. Everything hangs suspended for a moment, a look of "holy
shit" written on everybody's faces. Percy keeps yanking on the
big man's cuffs, leading him along with a cry of:

                              PERCY
                    Dead man walking! Dead man--

                              PAUL
                    Percy, that's enough.

Percy falls reproachfully silent. Paul doesn't dignify it,
just motions for them to come on. The procession comes down
the Mile, with Brutal and Dean bringing up the rear.

                              BRUTAL
                    You sure you wanna be in there
                    with him?

THE
GREEN
MILE

11

                                              (CONTINUED)

                         PAUL
                   (looks to Coffey)
              Am I gonna have trouble with you,
              big boy?

Coffey shakes his head slowly. Paul takes the clipboard of
transfer papers from Harry, turns and enters the cell.

Coffey just stands outside the cell and waits, as if he
doesn't understand the concept. Paul motions him to come on
in. Coffey starts to comply, but Percy raps him smartly with
the tip of his hickory baton to get him moving faster.

                         PERCY
              Move your ass.

Coffey flinches, enters the cell. Paul stares angrily at
Percy, who stands slapping his hickory baton against the palm
of his hand like a man with a toy he's itching to use.

                         PAUL
              Percy. They're moving house over
              in the infirmary. Why don't you go
              see if they could use some help?

                         PERCY
              They got all the men they need.

                         PAUL
              Why don't you just go make sure?
                   (off his look)
              I don't care where you go, Percy,
              as long as it's not here at this
              very moment.

Percy flushes red, the baton hovering near his palm. He looks
like he's about to say something, but thinks better of it and
stalks angrily up the Mile instead...

...and sees Del at his bars, smiling. Infuriated, Percy swings
his baton and smashes Del's fingers with a LOUD CRACK. Del
jerks back, howling in pain:

                         DEL
              OWW, GOD, HE BUS' MY FINGERS!

                         PERCY
              Wiped that grin off your shitpoke
              face, didn't I?

                         PAUL
              Goddamn it, Percy! Get the hell
              off my block!

Percy throws Paul a look of disdain -- your block, huh? He

THE
GREEN
MILE

12

                                        (CONTINUED)

swaggers out. Del's on his knees, weeping from the pain:

> DEL
> Oww, damn, boss, he done bus' my
> fingers for true...

> PAUL
> We'll get it looked at, Del, now
> keep yourself quiet like I said!

Del falls silent, moaning over his hand. Paul turns to Coffey, who looks unsettled by all the commotion.

> PAUL
> If I let Harry take those chains
> off you, you gonna be nice?

Coffey nods slowly. Harry enters to remove Coffey's shackles.

> PAUL
> Can you talk, big boy?

> COFFEY
> (deep and quiet)
> Yes sir, boss, I can talk.

> PAUL
> (checks clipboard)
> Your name is John Coffey?

> COFFEY
> Yes, sir, boss, like the drink,
> only not spelt the same.

> PAUL
> So you can spell, can you?

> COFFEY
> Jus' my name, boss.

> PAUL
> My name is Paul Edgecomb. If I'm
> not here, you can ask for Mr.
> Howell, Mr. Terwilliger, or Mr.
> Stanton...those gentlemen there.
> (beat)
> This isn't like the rest of the
> prison. It's a quiet place, we
> like to keep it that way.

Coffey considers this carefully, puzzled.

> COFFEY
> It weren't me making all the
> noise, boss.

THE
GREEN
MILE

13

> PAUL
> (eyes narrowing)
> You having a joke on me, John
> Coffey?

> COFFEY
> No, sir.

Paul sees he <u>isn't</u> joking, continues:

> PAUL
> Your time here can be easy or
> hard, depends on you. If you
> behave, you get to walk in the
> exercise yard every day. We might
> even play some music on the radio
> from time to time. Questions?

Coffey doesn't miss a beat, as if he's been waiting to ask:

> COFFEY
> Do you leave a light on after
> bedtime?

Paul blinks. It's the last thing he expected. Coffey smiles
uneasily, as if they might think him foolish for asking.

> COFFEY
> Because I get a little scared in
> the dark sometimes. If it's a
> strange place.

Paul looks to his men. The guards are trading glances.

> PAUL
> It's pretty bright in here all
> night long. We keep half the
> lights burning in the corridor.

> COFFEY
> Cor'der?

Coffey looks confused. Paul points to the lights lining the
ceiling of the Green Mile in wire mesh cages.

> PAUL
> Right out there.

Coffey nods, relieved. Then he surprises everybody by offering
his hand, as if to show proper manners. Paul hesitates, oddly
touched, then surprises his men even more by accepting.
Coffey's hand swallows his. A gentle handshake.

Paul steps from the cell. Brutal slides the door shut, locks
it. Coffey just stands there, waiting, unsure what to do.

(CONTINUED)

                    PAUL
          You can sit.

Coffey sinks onto the cot with his hands clasped between his
knees. He looks up at Paul, his voice soft as a whisper:

                    COFFEY
          Couldn't help it, boss. I tried to
          take it back, but it was too late.

Paul turns, leads his men up the Mile...

PAUL'S INNER OFFICE

...and they enter a few moments later. Paul is furious, but
keeping a lid on his temper:

                    PAUL
          Dean, soon as we're done here, run
          Delacroix up to the infirmary and
          see if his fingers are broken.

                    BRUTAL
          Course they're broken, I heard the
          damn bones crack. Goddamn Percy.

                    HARRY
          You hear what he was yelling when
          we brought the big dummy in?

                    PAUL
          How could I miss it, Harry? The
          whole prison heard.

                    BRUTAL
          You'll probably have to answer for
          sending him off the Mile. He's
          gonna cause you trouble over this,
          you mark me.

                    PAUL
          I'll chew that food when I have
          to. Right now I wanna hear about
          the new inmate...aside from how
          big he is, okay?

                    BRUTAL
               (smiles)
          Monstrous big. Damn.

                    DEAN
          Seems meek enough. Retarded, you
          figure?

                                              (CONTINUED)

> PAUL
> (nods)
> Looks like they sent us an
> imbecile to execute.

> HARRY
> Imbecile or not, he deserves to
> fry for what he done. Here...

Harry tosses a pair of manila envelopes bound with rubber
bands on the desk before Paul -- Coffey's file.

> HARRY
> ...make your blood curdle.

CUT TO:

EXT - E BLOCK PRISON YARD - DAY

A small area reserved for inmates of the Mile, fenced-off from
the main prison yard. Arlen Bitterbuck walks the perimeter
under the watchful eyes of guard BILL DODGE.

We find Paul sitting by himself on the bleachers with Coffey's
file on his knees, thoughtfully unwrapping his brown-bagged
sandwich. PUSH SLOWLY IN as he begins to read...

EXT - DETTERICK FARM - DAWN (FLASHBACK)

...and we see Klaus Detterick walk from his house to the barn
with a milking pail, a solitary figure against a brightening
horizon. He disappears into the barn...

...and we hold for a long moment, the house silent b.g.,
chickens clucking and scratching in the front yard...

...until a WOMAN'S SCREAM shatters the silence. Klaus
reappears, dropping the pail, running toward the house...

PAUL ON BLEACHERS

...as Paul turns the page, keeps reading...

INT - DETTERICK HOUSE - DAWN (FLASHBACK)

...and Klaus bursts in to find his wife MARJORIE absolutely
frantic with terror:

> KLAUS
> WHAT? GOD SAKES, WHAT?

> MARJORIE
> THE GIRLS! THE GIRLS ARE GONE!

(CONTINUED)

She drags him through the house to a screened-off porch area
where their 12 year-old son HOWIE is pointing and shouting --

                    HOWIE
          Papa! Papa, look! The blood!

-- and Klaus freezes there, stunned to see blood spattered on
the floor and the screen door hanging off its hinges...

                    KLAUS
          Oh my God.

PAUL ON BLEACHERS

...as Paul absently takes another bite of his sandwich, not
really tasting it, keeps reading...

INT - DETTERICK HOUSE - DAWN (FLASHBACK)

...plunging us back into screaming chaos: Klaus grabbing up
shotgun shells, Howie loading the .22 rifle he got for
Christmas, Marjorie sobbing incoherently...

                    KLAUS
          GODDAMN IT, WOMAN, GET ON THE PHONE
          NOW! YOU TELL 'EM WE HEADED WEST!
          MIND WHAT I'M SAYING! WEST, Y'HEAR?

...and she goes stumbling through the house, grabbing for the
phone as her men disappear toward the porch b.g.:

                    MARJORIE
          Central! Central, are you on the
          line? Oh, God, please, somebody
          took my little girls...

OUTSIDE THE HOUSE

Klaus and his son race from the house, following spatters of
blood across the yard...

PAUL ON BLEACHERS

...as Paul lets out a long breath, turns the page...

EXT - COUNTRY ROAD/FIELD - DAY (FLASHBACK)

...and we see CARS AND TRUCKS pulling up, MEN jumping out with
rifles, pouring down the incline toward the field where Klaus
is hollering and waving his arms. SHERIFF McGEE comes sliding
down from the road, taking charge. DOGS come bounding from the
back of a truck, howling down the incline to lead the chase...

THE
GREEN
MILE

17

                              (CONTINUED)

VARIOUS ANGLES

...which takes us through the cattails and bulrushes...to the
spot where Klaus finds the little scrap of pale yellow fabric,
turns and screams...

> KLAUS
> Oh, Lord, this belongs to my
> Katie...

...and they keep going, stopping abruptly as they find:
A blood-drenched area of trampled grass. A little girl's
bloody nightgown hangs in the low branches of a tree. Some of
these strong men look like they might throw up or faint at the
sight of it. Their blood freezes in their veins as an INHUMAN
HOWLING commences up ahead. It's like nothing they've ever
heard before, raising the hackles of men and dogs alike.

PAUL ON BLEACHERS

...as Paul quietly turns another page, shaking his head...

> PAUL
> Jesus.

EXT - FIELD - DAY (FLASHBACK)

The men reload their weapons. Everybody's terrified. McGee
starts off, the others following his lead toward --

THE RIVER

-- where they emerge from the treeline, drawing ever closer to
the source of that INHUMAN HOWLING...

...and they stop, gazing in horror:

John Coffey sits on the riverbank in bloody overalls, his huge
feet splayed out before him. He's making that inhuman howling
sound, face twisted in monstrous grief, pausing occasionally
to take in a great hitching breath of air.

Curled in his massive arms are the naked bodies of Detterick's
9 year-old twin girls, their once-blonde hair now matted to
their heads with blood.

A tableau. The men staring. John Coffey howling. A train
puffing smoke across the landscape.

Klaus Detterick breaks the moment, lunging down the riverbank
in a headlong rush. The others try to grab him, but he shrugs
them off and throws himself on Coffey with a scream of
inarticulate rage, kicking and punching, fists flying. Coffey
barely seems to notice.

(CONTINUED)

The others catch up with Klaus, drag him off. He falls to his
knees on the riverbank, sobbing into his hands. Howie runs to
him, throws himself into his father's arms. They hug each
other tightly, overwhelmed with grief.

A semblance of quiet descends, except for Coffey's heartbroken
wailing. A ring of rifle-toting men forms around him, though
he hardly seems aware of it. McGee steps forward, uncertain:

>   McGEE
>   Mister.

Coffey goes quiet at once, eyes still streaming tears.

>   McGEE
>   Mister? Can you hear me?
>   (Coffey nods)
>   You have a name?

>   COFFEY
>   John Coffey. Like the drink, only
>   not spelt the same.

McGee hunkers carefully down, watching for any sudden moves.

>   McGEE
>   What happened here, John Coffey?
>   You want to tell me that?

>   COFFEY
>   I couldn't help it. I tried to
>   take it back, but it was too late.

>   McGEE
>   (pause)
>   Boy, you are under arrest for
>   murder.

McGee spits in Coffey's face...

PAUL ON BLEACHERS

...as Paul looks up with a slight start, jarred from his
reading to find WARDEN HAL MOORES standing before him.

>   HAL
>   I interrupt?

>   PAUL
>   I'm just about done.

Paul stows the file as Hal settles onto the bleachers.

>   PAUL
>   How's that pretty gal of yours?

(CONTINUED)

                    HAL
        Melinda's not so well, Paul. Not
        so well at all. Got laid up with
        another headache yesterday. Worst
        one yet. She's also developed this
        weakness in her right hand.

                    PAUL
        Doctor still think it's migraines?

Hal gives a slight shake of his head.

                    HAL
        I'll be taking her up to Indianola
        next day or so for some tests. Head
        X-rays and the like. She is scared
        to death. Truth to tell, so am I.

                    PAUL
        If it's something they can see
        with an X-ray, maybe it's
        something they can fix.

                    HAL
        Maybe.

He pulls a letter, hands it to Paul.

                    HAL
        This just came in. D.O.E. on
        Bitterbuck.

Paul glances toward Bitterbuck, scans the letter, nods.

                    PAUL
        You didn't come all the way down
        here just to hand me a D.O.E.

                    HAL
        No. I had an angry call from the
        state capital about twenty minutes
        ago. Is it true you ordered Percy
        Wetmore off the block?

                    PAUL
        It is.

                    HAL
        I'm sure you had reason, Paul, but
        like it or not, the wife of the
        governor of this state has only
        one nephew, and his name happens
        to be Percy Wetmore. I need to
        tell you how this lays out?

                                        (CONTINUED)

PAUL
Little Percy called his aunt and
squealed like a schoolroom sissy.
(Hal nods)
He also mention he assaulted a
prisoner this morning out of sheer
petulance? Broke three fingers on
Eduard Delacroix's left hand?

HAL
I didn't hear that part. I'm sure
she didn't either.

PAUL
The man is mean, careless, and
stupid. Bad combination in a place
like this. Sooner or later, he's
gonna get somebody hurt. Or worse.

HAL
You and Brutus Howell will make
sure that doesn't happen.

PAUL
Easy enough to say. We can't watch
him every minute.

HAL
Stick with it, Paul. May not be
much longer. I have it on good
authority that Percy has an
application in at Briar Ridge.

PAUL
Briar Ridge? The mental hospital?

HAL
(nods)
Administration job. Better pay.

PAUL
Then why's he still here? He could
get that application pushed
through...hell, with his
connections, he could have any
state job he wants.

Hal has no answer. Paul looks off toward Bitterbuck.

PAUL
Tell you what I think. I think he
just wants to see one cook up
close.

Hal follows Paul's gaze, takes his meaning.

(CONTINUED)

                    HAL
          Well, he'll get his chance then,
          won't he? Maybe then he'll be
          satisfied and move on. In the
          meantime, you'll keep the peace?

                    PAUL
          Of course.

                    HAL
          Thank you, Paul.

Hal rises, slapping yard dust off his trousers.

                    PAUL
          Hal? You give Melinda my love,
          okay? I bet that X-ray turns out
          to be nothing at all.

Hal walks away looking like he's got the weight of the world
on his shoulders. Paul looks at the letter again...

TIGHT ON LETTER

...which is headed: "Date Of Execution."

                              DISSOLVE TO:

INT - PAUL'S HOUSE - NIGHT

Paul is at the kitchen table in the wee hours of the morning,
drinking buttermilk and listening to SOFT MUSIC on the radio.
JANICE EDGECOMB appears, shuffling sleepily downstairs.

                    JAN
          Paul?

                    PAUL
          Hey, you. Music too loud?

                    JAN
          No. There's just this big empty
          spot in the bed where my husband
          usually sleeps.

                    PAUL
          He said to tell you he's having a
          little trouble with that tonight.

She comes into the kitchen, strokes his hair. There's an easy
familiarity and a deep love between these two.

                    JAN
          Worried about Melinda and Hal? Is
          that what's got you up?

                                        (CONTINUED)

                         PAUL
               Yeah, that. Things.

                         JAN
               Things.

She sits on his lap and gives him a crooked smile -- you're
not getting off that easily.

                         PAUL
               Got a new inmate today. Big,
               simple-minded fella.

                         JAN
               Do I want to hear what he did?

                         PAUL
               No. One sleepless member of this
               family's enough.
                         (softly)
               The things that happen in this
               world. It's a wonder God allows it.

She gives him a tiny kiss above his left eyebrow, in that
special spot that makes him prickle.

                         JAN
               Why don't you come to bed? I've
               got something to help you sleep,
               and you can have all you want.

                         PAUL
               Don't I wish. I've still got
               something wrong with my waterworks,
               I don't want to pass it on to you.

                         JAN
               You seen Doc Bishop yet?

                         PAUL
               No, because he'll want me to take
               sulfa tablets and I'll spend the
               rest of the week puking in every
               corner of my office. It'll run its
               course all by itself, thank you
               very much for your concern.

She kisses that spot above his eyebrow again. He smiles.

                         JAN
               Poor old guy...

                                   DISSOLVE TO:

INT - EXECUTION CHAMBER - NIGHT

Maintenance time for Old Sparky. Paul is carefully sanding a
connector plug while Dean waxes the electric chair's wooden
arms to a gleam.

They pause, thinking they hear a LAUGH drifting in from E
Block...and then Brutal calls softly to them:

> BRUTAL (O.S.)
> Paul? Dean?

INT - E BLOCK - NIGHT

Paul and Dean enter to find Brutal trying not to wake the cons
in their cells by laughing too loudly. They follow his gaze
down the Mile, see nothing, turn to him like he's crazy.

> BRUTAL
> I guess the legislature loosened
> those purse-strings enough to hire
> on a new guard.
> > (off their looks)
> Look again. He's right there.

Paul and Dean look again, and this time they see it:

A tiny brown mouse is coming up the Mile. It trots a short
distance, peers right and left as if checking the snoring
inmates in their cells, then makes another forward spurt.

> PAUL
> He's doing a cell check.

This gets them all trying not to laugh. The mouse draws ever
closer. Dean starts to look worried.

> DEAN
> It ain't normal for a mouse to
> come up on people that way. Maybe
> it's rabid.

> BRUTAL
> Oh, my Christ. The big mouse
> expert. The Mouse Man. You see it
> foaming at the mouth, Mouse Man?

> DEAN
> > (dubious)
> I don't see its mouth at all.

That does it -- Paul and Brutal burst out laughing. The mouse
stops before them and peers up, curling its tail primly around
its paws as if to wait. The guards fall silent, fascinated.
Bitterbuck stirs in his cell, sits up to watch.

THE
GREEN
MILE

(CONTINUED)

Brutal tears off a piece of his half-eaten corned beef
sandwich, holds it delicately out with two fingers. The mouse
rises up, appraising the morsel with shiny black eyes.

> DEAN
> Aw, Brutal, no! We'll be hip-deep
> in mice around here...

> BRUTAL
> (to Paul)
> I just wanna see what he'll do. In
> the interests of science, like.

Paul shrugs. Brutal drops the scrap. The mouse grabs it and
eats, sitting up like a dog doing a trick. Bitterbuck mutters
from his cell:

> BITTERBUCK
> That's one smart mouse. Or just
> hungry as hell.

The mouse turns and scurries back down the Mile, vanishing
under the restraint room door at the far end. Dean throws Paul
an "I told you so" look.

> DEAN
> He's in the damn restraint room.
> You know he's gonna be chewing the
> padding out of the walls and
> making himself a nice little nest.

Brutal gives Paul a sheepish look -- well? Paul sighs.

> PAUL
> All right. Let's get the damn
> mouse.

They stride grimly down the Mile to the restraint room door,
men on a mission. Coffey's awake now, peering from his cot.

> COFFEY
> Saw me a mouse go by.

> PAUL
> It was a dream. Go back to sleep.

> COFFEY
> Weren't no dream. It was a mouse
> all right.

> PAUL
> Can't put anything over on you.

Paul unlocks the door, revealing a padded room filled with
storage: cleaning supplies, buckets of paint, mops and

THE
GREEN
MILE

(CONTINUED)

ladders, you name it. Brutal shrugs off his jacket. Paul grabs
a mop from a steel bucket, hands it to Dean.

                    PAUL
          Dean, watch the door. He tries to
          get past you, whack him.

                    DEAN
          Brutal or the mouse?

                    BRUTAL
          Har har, Mouse Man.

Brutal and Paul start doing the heavy lifting, muscling an
unused filing cabinet out the door...

                    DISSOLVE:

...and they finally relay the last few heavy buckets of paint
onto the Mile. Paul and Brutal catch their breath, scanning
the empty restraint room. Their eyes go glaringly to Dean.

                    PAUL
          You let him get past you.

                    DEAN
          No I didn't, I was here all the
          time!

                    BRUTAL
          Then where the hell is he?

They move slowly into the room, peering into every nook and
cranny, utterly mystified. Brutal shakes his head.

                    BRUTAL
          Three grown men. Outsmarted by a
          mouse.

                    DEAN
          Well, bright side is, all this
          commotion probably scared him off
          for good.

                    PAUL
          Yeah, that's right. That's the
          last we'll see of him...

                    FADE TO BLACK

IN BLACKNESS, A TITLE CARD APPEARS:

          "The Mouse on the Mile"

                    CUT TO:

INT - E BLOCK - DAY

A low, static shot. Green floor stretching before us. Harry and Bill Dodge are at the desk b.g., doing paperwork and filing chores. Percy is idling nearby, whistling softly and combing his hair...

...and into this quiet shot, deep in foreground, creeps the mouse. He starts walking the Mile as before...

...right toward Percy.

COFFEY

stares through his bars as the mouse goes by...

PERCY

keeps combing his hair, unaware...

DEL

sits quietly picking his nose in his cell. The mouse appears outside the bars, cruising inexorably up the Mile. Del turns slowly, watches the mouse go by...

PERCY

still grooming himself, still unaware...

THE MOUSE

keeps coming closer. ANGLE UP to Bitterbuck peering through his bars, watching him go by...

PERCY

keeps working that comb -- and freezes at the sound of a TINY SQUEAK. His head swivels slowly...

...and there's the mouse. Staring at him.

That moment of eye contact reveals an enmity older than time itself. If mice have a natural enemy, Percy is it.

                    PERCY
          You little son of a bitch.

Harry and Bill glance up from their work.

                    HARRY
          Well, I'll be damned. There he is,
          big as Billy-be-frigged. I thought
          Brutal was pulling my leg.

THE
GREEN
MILE

                              (CONTINUED)

                         BILL
              That's a goddamn mouse.

                         HARRY
              Yeah. Brute said he was in here
              last night begging for food, came
              right up to the desk.

                         BILL
              My ass. Give him some room, Percy,
              see what he does.

Percy takes a few careful steps back, eyes never leaving the
mouse. (Percy's hand starts easing toward the handle of his
baton.) The mouse comes up to the desk as before.

                         HARRY
              Brave little bastard, gotta give
              him that.

Harry breaks off a small piece of cracker and drops it. The
mouse picks it up, starts to eat. (Percy's hand inches ever
closer to his baton).

                         BILL
              Here, lemme try.

Bill drops a piece of cracker. The mouse ignores it
completely, keeping its beady little eyes on Harry. (Percy's
hand starts easing his baton from its holster.)

                         BILL
              Maybe he's full.

                         HARRY
                    (grins)
              Maybe he knows you're just a
              floater. Gotta be an E Block
              regular to feed the E Block mouse,
              don'cha know...

Harry drops another piece -- and sure enough, the mouse starts
to eat. Harry's smile fades. He and Bill trade a look.

                         HARRY
              I was just kidding ab--

Percy lets rip a BELLOWING WAR CRY ("Yaaaahhh!") and launches
his baton like a spear, scaring the crap out of everyone.

The mouse ducks (yes, actually ducks) and the baton sails over
his head close enough to ruffle its fur, bouncing off the
floor. Apparently remembering a pressing engagement elsewhere,
the mouse takes off in a flash toward the restraint room.

THE
GREEN
MILE

                                              (CONTINUED)

Percy roars with frustration and takes off after it, trying to
squash it with his heavy work shoes, leaping and stomping with
great big galloping strides, missing the mouse by inches...

...and thus is the Green Mile traversed, with Percy stomping
and hollering like a spastic flamenco dancer, the convicts
yelling at their bars, the mouse zigging and zagging like Jim
Thorpe heading for the endzone...

The mouse wins, zipping to safety under the restraint room
door. Percy pounds his fist against the door in frustration:

                    PERCY
          FUCK!

He fumbles his keys, unlocks the door, yelling all the while:

                    PERCY
          I'M GONNA RIP YOUR DISEASED HEAD
          OFF, YOU LITTLE PIECE OF SHIT!

OUTSIDE E BLOCK

Paul and Brutal are arriving for work -- they pause, hearing
PERCY'S YELLS drifting from the windows. The regular CONS in
the yard are drifting curiously to the fence, wondering if a
riot's brewing. Paul and Brutal take off running --

INSIDE E BLOCK

-- and rush in to find:

                    HARRY
          Percy met your mouse.

Harry points. Percy's down at the far end, rummaging wildly in
the restraint room, tossing shit out onto the Mile.

                    PERCY
          It's in here somewhere! I'm gonna
          squish the little son of a bitch!

He starts muscling the filing cabinet out the door, kicking
buckets out of his way. Brutal calls to him:

                    BRUTAL
          Percy, we already tried that--

                    PERCY
          What? Whad'ja say?

                    BRUTAL
          I said--

Paul stops Brutal with a look -- don't you dare stop him.

                                        (CONTINUED)

                    BRUTAL
          --uh, knock yourself out. Hope you
          nail the bastard.

Paul crosses his arms and smiles, leans back against the desk
to wait...

                    DISSOLVE:

...and Percy hauls the last of the stuff out, exhausted. He
steps back in and looks around, unable to believe there's no
mouse cowering in the corner. Paul and the men approach,
keeping straight faces, navigating the crap in the corridor.

                    BRUTAL
          Gosh. Ain't in there, huh? Don't
          that beat the mousie band?

Percy keeps scanning the restraint room. The others all look
to Paul, waiting for him to speak -- you're the boss.

                    PAUL
          Percy. You want to think about
          what you were doing just now.

                    PERCY
               (turns, glaring)
          I know what I was doing. Trying
          to get the mouse. You blind?

                    HARRY
          You also scared the living crap
          out of me and Bill. And them.

He cocks a thumb at the inmates in their cells.

                    PERCY
          So what? They aren't in cradle-
          school, case you didn't notice...
               (directed at Paul)
          ...although you treat them that
          way half the time.

                    BRUTAL
          We don't scare 'em any more than
          we have to, Percy. They're under
          enough strain as it is.

                    PAUL
          Men under strain can snap. Hurt
          themselves. Hurt others. That's
          why our job is talking, not
          yelling. You'll do better to think
          of this place like an intensive
          care ward in a hospital--

                                        (CONTINUED)

                         PERCY
          I think of it as a bucket of piss
          to drown rats in. That's all.
                    (scans their faces)
          Anybody doesn't like it can kiss
          my ass. How's that sit?

Brutal steps forward, wanting to slug the little bastard.
Percy shies back, but keeps his bravado up:

                         PERCY
          Try it. You'll be on the bread
          lines before the week is out.

                         PAUL
          We all know who your connections
          are, Percy...
                    (steps close)
          ...but you ever threaten a man on
          this block again, we're all gonna
          have a go. Job be damned.

                         PERCY
          Big talk. You done?

                         PAUL
          Get all this shit back in the
          restraint room. You're cluttering
          up my Mile.

They turn and walk away, leaving Percy as we

                                   DISSOLVE TO:

INT - E BLOCK - NIGHT

A SLOW TRACKING SHOT OF THE GREEN FLOOR takes us past a tiny
scrap of bread...and then another scrap...and then past a
mousetrap primed with a scrap of bacon...

...and we keep following a long trail of bread scraps and
mousetraps until we come to Percy, alone on the Mile,
carefully laying the last mousetrap down...

...and he scoots back against the desk to wait, crouched and
holding his breath, eyes riveted to the restraint room door
for any sign of his furry nemesis...

...and CAMERA BOOMS SLOWLY DOWN off his face, dipping down to
floor level...

...where the mouse is revealed under the desk, peering in the
same direction as Percy, wondering what the hell's so
interesting down there. It hops further out to see...

THE
GREEN
MILE

31

                                             (CONTINUED)

ANGLE OF PERCY FROM FLOOR LEVEL

...and the mouse enters frame, hopping out a few more steps, mouse and man staring in the same direction.

A long beat. Percy turns, looks down at the mouse. The mouse turns, looks up at Percy...

...and all hell breaks loose again. They race the Mile as before, Percy hollering and stomping all the way, mousetraps snapping and flying up into frame as they go charging wildly past the cells.

The mouse wins again. Percy pauses, furious...and sees Coffey staring at him from his cell.

                    COFFEY
          Saw me a mouse go by.

Percy loses it, kicking and punching the restraint room door in a screaming rage as we

                              FADE TO:

INT - E BLOCK - DAY

Paul appears at Bitterbuck's bars with a group of guards.

                    PAUL
          Arlen? Your daughter and her
          family are here.

Bitterbuck steps from the cell. Bill Dodge escorts him off the block. The moment they're gone:

                    PAUL
          Let's move. I want at least two
          rehearsals before he gets back.

INT - VISITOR'S ROOM - DAY

Bitterbuck is led in. His DAUGHTER rises...an awkward hesitation...and she touches his face, kisses him. He takes her hands, kisses them, tries not to cry. The rest of the family is there: SON-IN-LAW, GRANDCHILDREN, COUSINS. They form around him, murmuring hellos, shaking hands...

INT - E BLOCK - DAY

...while TOOT-TOOT, a wiry old trusty, takes Bitterbuck's place in the cell.

                    TOOT
          Sittin' down, sittin' down,
          rehearsing now! Everybody settle!

                                        (CONTINUED)

He glances to Paul -- okay, hit it.

                    PAUL
          Arlen Bitterbuck, step forward.

Toot springs to his feet and steps from the cell.

                    TOOT
          I'm steppin' forward, I'm steppin'
          forward, I'm steppin' forward...

Toot turns, shows the top of his head to Dean.

                    PAUL
          Is his head properly shaved?

                    DEAN
          No, it's dandruffy and it smells.

                    PAUL
          I'll take that for a yes. All
          right, Arlen, let's go.

Toot starts up the corridor, ringed by guards.

                    TOOT
          I'm walkin' the Mile, I'm walkin'
          the Mile, I'm walkin' the Mile...

PAUL'S INNER OFFICE

Toot throws himself to his knees as soon as they enter:

                    TOOT
          I'm prayin', I'm prayin', I'm
          prayin'. The Lord is my shepherd,
          so on an' so forth...

                    PAUL
          Toot, you have to wait till I tell
          you to pray.
               (Toot waits)
          Okay, pray.

                    TOOT
          Still prayin', still prayin'...

                    HARRY
          Paul, we're not gonna have some
          Cherokee medicine man in here
          whoopin' and hollerin' and shaking
          his dick, are we?

                    PAUL
          Well, actually--

THE
GREEN
MILE

33

> TOOT
> Still prayin', prayin', gettin'
> right with Jesus...

> HARRY
> Do it quietly, you old gink!

Harry slaps Toot upside the head to shut him up.

> PAUL
> As I was saying, I don't believe
> they actually shake their dicks,
> Harry. Be that as it may, Mr.
> Bitterbuck is a Christian, so we
> got Reverend Schuster coming in.

> DEAN
> Oh, he's good. Fast, too. Doesn't
> get 'em worked up.

> PAUL
> On your feet, Toot. You've prayed
> enough for one day.

> TOOT
> Gettin' to my feet, walkin' again,
> walkin' on the Green Mile...

EXECUTION CHAMBER

They enter. Brutal is waiting for them, gun drawn. Percy peers
out from behind the partition wall from the switch room.

> PERCY
> What do I do?

> PAUL
> Watch and learn.

Paul motions Percy behind the wall. Percy sighs, takes his
spot next to Jack Van Hay, peers through the wire mesh as Toot
plops into Old Sparky, wriggling his skinny ass to get comfy.

> TOOT
> Sittin' down, sittin' down, takin'
> a seat in Old Sparky's lap...

Paul and Dean kneel to apply the ankle clamps. Brutal steps in
from the side, pressing down on the condemned man's left arm
to keep him in place until the ankle clamps are secure. Harry
moves in from the other side, securing the right arm clamp.

> TOOT
> Gettin' clamped, gettin' clamped,
> gettin'--ow, shit, watch the skin.

(CONTINUED)

Paul signals "ankles secure." Brutal holsters his pistol, applies the final clamp to the left arm.

> BRUTAL
> Roll on one.

BEHIND THE PARTITION

Van Hay mimes turning the generator knob up, whispering:

> VAN HAY
> "Roll on one" means I turn the
> generator up full. You'll see the
> lights go brighter in half the
> prison...

RESUME MAIN CHAMBER

as Brutal steps before the "condemned" and pronounces:

> BRUTAL
> Arlen Bitterbuck, you have been
> condemned to die by a jury of your
> peers, sentence imposed by a judge
> in good standing in this state. Do
> you have anything to say before
> the sentence is carried out?

> TOOT
> (gleefully)
> Yeah! I want a fried chicken
> dinner with gravy on the taters, I
> want to shit in your hat, and I
> got to have Mae West sit on my
> face, because I am one horny
> motherfucker!

Brutal tries to hold on, but it's impossible -- he cracks up. Everybody falls apart, howling helplessly with laughter. Even Jack Van Hay is guffawing behind his partition.

Only Paul is reining it in -- he's a little too pissed to go with it. He waits until the laughing fit starts to pass, then:

> PAUL
> Shut up, Brutal. That goes for
> everybody. I want quiet in here.
> (turns)
> Toot, another remark like that,
> I'll have Van Hay roll on two for
> real.

> BRUTAL
> (beat, gently)
> It _was_ pretty funny.

THE
GREEN
MILE

35

(CONTINUED)

                    PAUL
          That's why I don't like it.
          Tomorrow night we're doing this
          for real. I don't want somebody
          remembering a stupid joke like
          that and getting going again.
                  (off their looks)
          Ever try not laughing in church
          once something funny gets stuck in
          your head? Same goddamn thing.

                    BRUTAL
          Sorry, Paul. You're right. Let's
          keep going. Harry...

Harry takes a black mask and snugs it down over Toot's head,
leaving only the crown of his head exposed. Brutal takes a
large sponge, dips it in a steel bucket, mimes soaking it...

BEHIND THE PARTITION

                    PERCY
          What's with the sponge?

                    VAN HAY
          You soak it in brine, get it good
          and wet. Conducts the electricity
          directly to the brain, fast like a
          bullet. You don't ever throw the
          switch on a man without that.

RESUME MAIN CHAMBER

as the sponge is placed atop Toot's head. Harry now lowers the
steel cap and Brutal secures the straps.

                    BRUTAL
          Arlen Bitterbuck, electricity
          shall now be passed through your
          body until you are dead, in
          accordance with state law. God
          have mercy on your soul.
                  (to Van Hay)
          Roll on two.

BEHIND THE PARTITION

Van Hay mimes flipping the switch, looks to Percy:

                    VAN HAY
          And that's that.

RESUME MAIN CHAMBER

Toot can't resist -- he starts bucking and flailing:

                                              (CONTINUED)

                    TOOT
          Now I'm fryin'! Fryin'! Geeaaah!
          Fryin' like a done tom turkey!

Paul rolls his eyes at Brutal. Brutal shifts his gaze past
him and nods -- look behind you.

                    BRUTAL
          One of the witnesses showed up a
          day early.

Paul turns. Sitting on the door sill, watching them with beady
eyes, is the mouse. Paul turns back, addresses the room:

                    PAUL
          All right, let's go again and do
          it right this time! Get that idiot
          out of the chair...

HIGH WIDE ANGLE OF EXECUTION CHAMBER

Brutal and Harry start undoing Toot's clamps. Everybody
relaxes, drifting from their positions...

                              DISSOLVE TO:

SAME ANGLE AS ABOVE - NEXT NIGHT

...and the room is now quietly filling up with WITNESSES
trickling in. People speak in whispers, if at all.

INT - BITTERBUCK'S CELL - NIGHT

Dean is performing some focused task, his concentration great.
We're hearing GENTLE SCRAPING SOUNDS. ANGLE TILTS DOWN...

...past the gleaming straight-razor he's using to carefully
shave the top of somebody's head...

...to reveal Bitterbuck in TIGHT CLOSEUP, sitting very still.

Dean finishes, exits the cell. ANGLE SHIFTS to Paul sitting
with Bitterbuck. Bitterbuck runs his fingers lightly over the
newly-shaved spot on his head. Strange sensation. Softly:

                    BITTERBUCK
          You think if a man sincerely
          repents on what he done wrong, he
          might get to go back to the time
          that was happiest for him and live
          there forever? Could that be what
          heaven is like?

Paul doesn't think so -- but that's not what Bitterbuck needs
to hear, so the lie comes easy:

THE
GREEN
MILE

37

                                        (CONTINUED)

>PAUL
>I just about believe that very thing.

Pause. Bitterbuck smiles.

>BITTERBUCK
>Had me a young wife when I was
>eighteen. Spent our first summer
>in the mountains. Made love every
>night. She'd just lie there after,
>bare-breasted in the firelight,
>and we'd talk sometimes till the
>sun come up.
>>(beat)
>That was my best time.

Brutal appears at the door, checks his pocketwatch, nods to
Paul. Bitterbuck takes a deep breath, getting himself ready.

>PAUL
>It'll be fine. You'll do fine.

INT - EXECUTION CHAMBER - NIGHT

THE SPONGE is pulled sopping wet from the bucket of brine,
dripping a trail of water across the floor. Brutal places it
atop Bitterbuck's head. Water courses down the sides of the
condemned man's mask and neck, pooling on the floor.

The cap is lowered, the straps secured. All we hear now is the
sound of Bitterbuck's BREATHING growing louder and faster
under the mask...until, softly:

>BRUTAL
>Roll on two.

WHAM! The switch is thrown. Bitterbuck surges forward against
the straps, riding the powerful current.

Some witnesses turn away. Paul and Brutal maintain grim eye
contact with each other, waiting.

Behind the partition, Percy watches through the mesh with
gleaming eyes, wishing he could see better.

Van Hay kills the current. Bitterbuck goes limp. A DOCTOR
steps forward, checks for a heartbeat, shakes his head.

>BRUTAL
>Again.

The switch is thrown a second time. Bitterbuck surges forward
again, riding the current all the way...

>CUT TO:

INT - E BLOCK ACCESS TUNNEL - NIGHT

Bitterbuck's dead face stares up at us from a gurney. A hand reaches down, gives his cheek a squeeze. TILT UP to:

>   PERCY
>   Adios, Chief. Drop us a card from
>   hell, let us know if it's hot
>   enough.

Brutal knocks Percy's hand away, shoves him aside.

>   BRUTAL
>   He's paid what he owed. He's
>   square with the house again, so
>   keep your goddamn hands off him.

He draws the sheet over Bitterbuck's face, wheels the gurney down the tunnel. Percy throws a look to Paul.

>   PERCY
>   What's up his ass?

>   PAUL
>   You, Percy. Always you.

>   PERCY
>   You gotta hate the new boy? That
>   the way it is around here?

>   PAUL
>   Why not just move on? Go to Briar
>   Ridge.
>   (off his look)
>   Yeah, I know about it. Sounds like
>   a good job.

>   PERCY
>   I might take it, too. Soon as you
>   put me out front.

Paul cocks his head -- excuse me?

>   PERCY
>   You heard me. I want Brutal's
>   spot for the next execution.

>   PAUL
>   What's with you? Seeing a man die
>   isn't enough? You gotta be close
>   enough to smell his nuts cook?

>   PERCY
>   I wanna be out front, is all. Just
>   one time. Then you'll be rid of me.

THE GREEN MILE

(CONTINUED)

> PAUL
> If I say no?

> PERCY
> I might just stick around for good,
> make me a career of this. Boss.

Paul just shakes his head in wonder and walks away.

> FADE TO:

INT - COFFEY'S CELL - DAY

Coffey's lying on his bunk, eyes leaking quiet tears. He stirs
at the sound of GIGGLING. He sits up, peers curiously through
the bars. Softly:

> COFFEY
> Del?

AT THE GUARD STATION

Paul glances up from writing in the daily log. Silence now.
He goes back to writing -- and the GIGGLING comes again.

> PAUL
> Delacroix? That you?

No answer. Just more giggling. Paul rises, walks down the Mile
to Delacroix's cell -- and stops, staring in through the bars.

PAUL'S INNER OFFICE

Brutal and Dean are having lunch. Paul pokes his head in.

> PAUL
> You are not gonna believe this.

RESUME E BLOCK

The men follow Paul onto the Mile. By now, Del is CACKLING
WILDLY in his cell. Brutal shoots Paul a look -- has he gone
insane? Paul gestures "see for yourself."

They arrive at the bars...and find the mouse sitting on Del's
shoulder. Del looks up, giggling like a kid at Christmas.

> DEL
> Look! I done tame me dat mouse!

> PAUL
> We see that.

> DEL
> Watch dis! Watch what he do!

(CONTINUED)

He stretches out both arms. The creature scampers up one arm,
around the back of his neck, and travels all the way down the
other arm. The guards just stand there, staring.

>   DEL
>   Ain't he sumpthin now? Ain't Mr.
>   Jingles smart?

>   PAUL
>   Mr. Jingles?

>   DEL
>   Dat his name. He whisper it in my
>   ear. Cap'n, can I have a box for
>   my mouse so he can sleep in here
>   wi' me?

>   PAUL
>   I notice your English gets better
>   when you want something.

>   DEL
>   Wanna see what else he do? Watch,
>   watch, watch...

He puts the mouse on the floor, grabs a small wooden spool.
The mouse sees it, poises like a man getting ready for a race.

>   DEL
>   We play fetch, Mr. Jingles? We
>   play fetch?

He tosses the spool across the floor, bounces it against the
wall. The mouse goes after it like a dog after a stick -- and
proceeds to push it back to the bunk, rolling it with its
front paws all the way to Delacroix's foot.

By now, the guards' jaws are hanging open. Paul's got a funny
little chill running up his spine.

>   DEL
>   He fetch it ever' time. Smart as
>   hell, ain't he? We do da trick
>   again, watch, watch, watch...

Again he throws the spool. Again the mouse goes after it,
starts rolling it back. Del howls with laughter, claps his
hands like a kid. Brutal murmurs to the others:

>   BRUTAL
>   Who's training who here?

>   COFFEY
>   That's some smart mouse, Del. Like
>   he's a circus mouse or something.

THE
GREEN
MILE

41

(CONTINUED)

                         DEL
              A circus mouse! Dat jus' what he
              is, too! A circus mouse! I get
              outta here, he make me rich, see
              if he don't!

He picks up the spool again, makes a drumroll sound, tosses
it. The mouse does its thing, rolling the spool back...

...as Percy enters the scene. Del catches sight of him and
scoops up his mouse, drawing fearfully back on his bunk. He
tries to hide Mr. Jingles in his hands -- but the mouse
wriggles from his grasp and scampers up on his shoulder, where
he regards Percy with mistrustful, beady mouse eyes.

                         PERCY
              Well, well. Looks like you found
              yourself a new friend, Del.

Del tries to offer some defiance -- but all he can manage is:

                         DEL
              Don' hurt him, 'kay? 'kay?

Percy shrugs as if to say "no skin off me," looks to Paul.

                         PERCY
              That the one I chased?

                         PAUL
              Yes, that's the one. Only Del says
              his name is Mr. Jingles.

                         PERCY
              Is that so?

Paul trades a look with the others, everybody wondering just
what the hell's going through Percy's mind.

                         PAUL
              Del was just asking for a box. He
              thinks the mouse will sleep in it,
              I guess. That he might keep it for
              a pet. What do you think?

                         PERCY
              I think it'll shit up his nose
              some night and run away, but I
              guess that's Del's lookout.
                   (beat)
              We oughtta find a cigar box. Get
              some cotton batting from the
              dispensary to line it with. That
              should do real nice.

                                              (CONTINUED)

Percy walks away, leaving them dumbstruck. Paul turns to the others. Of all the things they've seen in the last few minutes, Percy being nice is the most amazing of all.

                    PAUL
          Man said get a cigar box.

                              CUT TO:

INT - PRISON ADMINISTRATION BUILDING - DAY

Paul comes up the stairs to the warden's office...

INT - WARDEN MOORES' OFFICE - DAY

...and enters to find Hal staring out the window.

                    PAUL
          Hal? You wanted to see me?

                    HAL
          Yeah. Paul. Close the door.

Hal's speech is halting, his thoughts disjointed and slow:

                    HAL
          Uh. So you know. You got a new
          prisoner coming in tomorrow.
          William Wharton. Young kid. Wild
          as hell, judging from this...

He picks up the report, trying to focus his thoughts:

                    HAL
          ...been rambling all over the
          state last few years, causing all
          kinds of trouble. Finally hit the
          big time. Killed three people in a
          holdup, including a pregnant
          woman. Got "Billy the Kid"
          tattooed on his left arm...bad
          news all around...

He trails off, no longer able to focus on the words. Paul is shocked to see tears spill silently down his cheeks.

                    PAUL
          Hal?

                    HAL
          It's a tumor, Paul. A brain tumor.

Paul doesn't know what to say. Hal looks at him.

THE
GREEN
MILE

                                        (CONTINUED)

> HAL
> They got X-ray pictures of it.
> It's the size of a lemon, they
> said, and way down deep inside
> where they can't operate. I
> haven't told her. I can't think
> how. For the life of me, Paul, I
> can't think how to tell my wife
> she's going to die.

Hal Moores, one of the toughest and steadiest men you'd ever meet, starts to cry. He dissolves into great big gasping sobs, losing all control.

                                        CUT TO:

INT - PAUL'S BEDROOM - NIGHT

Paul lies awake, watching Jan sleep. He looks troubled -- not to mention feverish. It occurs to him how badly he has to pee. He sits up, clutching at a queasy stab of pain in his groin...

LIVING ROOM STAIRS

...and comes hurrying down the steps, clutching himself...

EXT - HOUSE - NIGHT

...and he's moving even faster as he exits the kitchen, racing for the outhouse. He realizes he's not going to make it, stops to piss near the woodpile stacked against the shed...

...and as he does, he's hit with the most stunning pain of his life. He buckles to his knees -- it's only his flailing hand against the woodpile that prevents him from going face-first into his own piss. He crams his other hand to his mouth in an enormous effort not to scream and wake his wife.

He manages to ride it out until his bladder empties. He falls onto his side, rolls over on the grass, and stares up at the sky with both hands pressed to his groin.

                    PAUL
          ...oh God...oh God...

                                    FADE TO BLACK

IN BLACKNESS, A TITLE CARD APPEARS:

                "Coffey's Hands"

                                        CUT TO:

INT - PAUL'S KITCHEN - MORNING

Paul looks feverish and clammy as he buttons up his uniform
jacket. Jan is packing his lunch, throwing him looks, knowing
how sick he is.

                    PAUL
          I'm going.

                    JAN
          What?

                    PAUL
          To the doctor. I'm going.
               (off her look)
          Today. Just as soon as we get the
          new inmate squared away.

                    JAN
          That bad?

                    PAUL
          Oh yeah.

She hands him his brown-bagged lunch, kisses his face.

                                        CUT TO:

INT - BRIAR RIDGE MENTAL HOSPITAL - MORNING

We see a tattoo: "Billy the Kid." TILT UP to WILLIAM WHARTON
staring out the window, wearing a hospital gown, his face
utterly blank. He looks heavily medicated.

Harry, Dean, and Percy enter. Billy doesn't react, just keeps
staring out. Harry waves his fingers in Billy's face.

                    HARRY
          Boy's doped to the gills. Dean,
          hand me them clothes...

Dean relays some folded prison clothes to Harry.

                    HARRY
          William Wharton? Hey! I'm talking
          to you! Put these clothes on!

Billy turns with a vacant look, takes the clothes. He fumbles
with the shirt, drops the pants. Harry and Dean sigh. They
strip Billy's hospital gown off and proceed to put the shirt
on him, guiding his limp arms through the sleeves.

                    PERCY
          Hellraiser, huh? Looks more like a
          limp noodle to me. Hey! Hey, you!

THE
GREEN
MILE
─────
45

                                   (CONTINUED)

Billy looks up, meets Percy's eyes.

> PERCY
> You been declared competent! Know
> what that means? Means you're
> gonna ride the lightning, son!

Percy does a quick impression of a man jittering and jerking in the electric chair.

> PERCY
> Bzzzzzzzzt-zap! Just like that!
> How's it feel to know you're gonna
> die with your knees bent?

> DEAN
> C'mon, Percy, give us a hand.

Laughing, Percy picks up the pants. They proceed to help Billy into them one leg at a time...

> CUT TO:

INT - E BLOCK TOILET - DAY

Paul is trying to piss. Except for a few drops hitting the bowl, excruciating pain seems to be the only result. He gives up, grabs a towel, wipes the sweat from his feverish face...

INT - E BLOCK - DAY

...and steps gingerly from the toilet. Del's watching.

> DEL
> Don' look so good, boss. Look like
> you runnin' you a fever.

Paul shoots him a baleful look -- no kidding. Another voice calls softly from further down the Mile:

> COFFEY (O.S.)
> Boss Edgecomb? Needs ta see you
> down here, boss.

> PAUL
> Got things to tend to just now,
> John Coffey. You be still in your
> cell now, y'hear?

Coffey falls silent. Paul goes to the entrance door and peers through the viewing slot, anxious to have this over with...

EXT - COLD MOUNTAIN PENITENTIARY - DAY

The prison truck appears, swaying along the rutted road...

(CONTINUED)

IN THE TRUCK

...while Billy Wharton stares at nothing, drool dripping from his slack mouth in long strings.

INT - E BLOCK - DAY

Paul watches the truck pull in. He draws away from the slot, proceeds toward an empty cell...

ANGLE ON TRUCK

The rear doors are swung open. Harry emerges. Dean and Percy are guiding Billy by the arms, helping him down...

INSIDE E BLOCK

Paul waits at the empty cell. ANGLE PANS TIGHT to Coffey at his bars, eyes widening in a blossoming of some nameless fear or dread. Something bad's coming. A whisper:

> COFFEY
> Careful.

OUTSIDE E BLOCK

Billy is brought to the door. Dean pulls his keys, starts to unlock it. We PUSH IN on Billy's face, where the tiniest trace of a smile is starting to grow...

INSIDE E BLOCK

...and Coffey's unease grows with it. He presses his face to the bars, his whispering becoming more urgent:

> COFFEY
> Careful. Careful.

Paul hears him, glances back with a puzzled look. Coffey's gaze is directed at the door, which is being unlocked...

THE DOOR

...and opened. In that moment, the slack look on Billy's face gives way to a wild grin. A CRAZED SCREECH leaps from his throat, a cross between a rebel yell and a dog being tortured, freezing everybody's blood in their veins --

> BILLY
> Yeeeeeehaaaawwwwwwrooooo!

-- and he drops his wrist-chain down over Dean's head, jerks it tight, begins to strangle him. Dean lurches forward, Billy riding/propelling him through the door onto the Mile.

THE
GREEN
MILE

(CONTINUED)

Percy stands frozen in the doorway, stunned. Harry shoves him aside and jumps on Billy from behind, trying to get him off Dean. Dean is choking, turning purple.

Paul rushes from the cell to join the fray. <u>Billy whirls, delivering a stunning kick to Paul's groin.</u> Paul's bladder pain goes nuclear -- he falls back in agony, clutching himself and sucking air through his teeth, unable even to scream.

Billy rams an elbow into Harry's face, knocks him sprawling on the desk, screaming and laughing and howling all the while:

> BILLY
> WHOOOEE, BOYS! AIN'T THIS A PARTY,
> NOW? IS IT, OR WHAT?

Paul forces himself to his feet, pulls his revolver, draws down on Billy...

> PAUL
> LET HIM GO!

...but Billy jerks Dean around, using him as a shield...

> BILLY
> G'WAN, SHOOT! SEE WHO YA HIT!

Dean is choking, dying. Paul is shifting his aim, trying for a clear shot, not getting one. Percy's still just inside the doorway, pressed against the wall with fear...

> PAUL
> HIT HIM, PERCY! GODDAMN IT, HIT
> HIM!

> BILLY
> C'MON, PERCY, HIT ME! HIT ME, YOU
> LIMP NOODLE, HIT ME! YEEHAWWW!

...and suddenly a hand comes in, grabs the hickory stick out of Percy's grasp, raises it high --

-- <u>it's Brutal coming through the door.</u> He swings the baton and lands an awesome blow to Billy's head -- <u>THUMP!</u> The force of it spins Billy off his feet and slams him flat on his back.

Dean crawls away, gulping ragged breaths of air. Amazingly, Billy's still conscious -- he looks up at Brutal and laughs:

> BILLY
> Big fucker. Snuck up on me. No fair.

Still laughing, he makes another grab at Dean. Brutal whacks him again, turning his lights out for good. Brutal drops to Dean's side, helping him hack air back into his lungs:

(CONTINUED)

                    BRUTAL
          Breathe...breathe...that's it...

Everybody's reining in their adrenalin. Paul glares at Harry.

                    HARRY
          We thought he was doped.
               (to Percy)
          Didn't we? Didn't we all of us
          think he was doped?

Percy nods, still numb. Paul is furious:

                    PAUL
          You didn't <u>ask?</u> I guess that's not
          a mistake you'll be needing to
          make again anytime soon, is it?

Harry shakes his head miserably. Paul grabs Billy by the feet.

                    PAUL
          Grab his arms! You too, Percy!
               (off Percy's hesitation)
          Percy, goddamn it, get your feet out
          of cement and help us out here!

Percy finally unfreezes. The three of them hoist Billy up in a
dead-lift, get him in his cell, toss him on the cot. They step
out, slam the door, lock it. Paul looks to Harry and Brutal.

                    PAUL
          Get Dean looked at right away,
          make sure he's all right. Percy,
          you go make a report to the warden
          for me. Start off by saying the
          situation is under control -- it's
          not a story, he won't appreciate
          you drawing out the suspense.

                    BRUTAL
          What about you? You look about
          ready to collapse.

                    PAUL
          I've got the Mile till you all get
          back. Go on, now.

They all exit. As soon as he's alone, Paul gives in to the
pain, holding his crotch and sinking to his knees with a moan.
It's so bad he actually lays down on the Mile, face pressed
against the cool linoleum, wishing he were dead. A stretch of
silence...and then:

                    COFFEY (O.S.)
          Boss? Needs ta see ya down here.

THE
GREEN
MILE

49

                              (CONTINUED)

                    PAUL
          This is not a good time, John
          Coffey. Not a good time at all.

                    COFFEY (O.S.)
          But I needs ta see ya, boss. I
          needs ta talk t'ya.

Paul sighs. Things couldn't get much worse than this. He rises
with a supreme effort, walks painfully down the Mile...

COFFEY'S CELL

...and finds Coffey waiting at his bars.

                    COFFEY
          Closer.

                    PAUL
          I'm alone here right now, John.
          Figure this is close enough.

                    COFFEY
          Boss, please. I got to whisper in
          your ear.

Paul blinks. Maybe it's the fever clouding his brain, or
maybe...hell, is this what being hypnotized is like? He tries
to shake the sensation off, comes a little closer.

                    DEL
          Boss? You know you not s'pose to
          do dat.

                    PAUL
          Mind your business, Del. What do
          you want, John Coffey?

                    COFFEY
          Just to help.

His hand shoots out, grabs Paul by the collar, jerks him
close. Paul makes a panic-grab for his revolver...

...but Coffey lays his free hand atop Paul's, eases his grip
from the gun -- no need for that. Coffey's hand then drifts
slowly down, easing to Paul's crotch...

                    PAUL
                (stunned, frozen)
          What are you...doing?

...and something goes WHUMP through Paul's body. He arches
back with his mouth agape and arms outstretched as a rush of
energy seems to pass from Paul through Coffey's hand...

...and then it's over. Paul comes back to the real world, weak against the bars, realizes Del is hollering in his cell:

> DEL
> HELP! HELP! JOHN COFFEY'S KILLING
> BOSS EDGECOMB! HELP!

> PAUL
> Del, Chrissake, settle down, I'm
> fine...

It dawns on him that he really <u>is</u> fine. Fever's gone. So is the pain in his groin. John Coffey, though, seems to be having trouble. He sits down on his bunk and bends forward, gagging like a man with a chicken bone caught in his throat.

> PAUL
> John? John, what's wrong?

Paul fumbles his keys to the lock, unsure if he should open the door, watching the big man's contortions grow stronger like a cat trying to cough up a hairball...

...and then comes an unpleasant, gagging/retching sound as Coffey's lips draw back from his teeth in a kind of godawful sneer...<u>and he exhales a cloud of what look like tiny black insects.</u> They swirl furiously in front of his face, turn white...and disappear. Paul just stares, stunned. Softly:

> PAUL
> What did you do, big boy? What did
> you do to me?

> COFFEY
> I helped it. Didn't I help it?

> PAUL
> Yes, but...<u>how?</u>

Coffey shrugs -- it's something that just <u>is.</u>

> COFFEY
> Just took it back, is all. Awful
> tired now, boss. Dog tired.

He rolls onto his bunk, faces the wall. Paul just stares at him, stunned. He turns and walks up the Mile, his stiffness and pain now gone. Del watches him go by, also stunned:

> DEL
> What dat man do to you? He throw
> some gris-gris on you?
> (off Paul's look)
> You look diff'int! Even walk
> diff'int! Like y'all better!

THE
GREEN
MILE

(CONTINUED)

> PAUL
> You're imagining things. Lie down,
> Del. Get you some rest.

Paul continues up the Mile...

E BLOCK TOILET

...and steps back into the toilet. Not trusting this situation
for even a moment, Paul opens his fly, takes a deep breath to
prepare himself for the pain, starts to pee...

...and we hear a healthy stream of water hitting the bowl. The
look on Paul's face says it all -- blessed relief.

> CUT TO:

INT - PAUL'S HOUSE - DUSK

Paul comes home from work, still looking numb about the whole
thing. He drifts to the kitchen door. Jan's at the counter,
slicing vegetables for dinner. She glances at him.

> JAN
> Hi, honey. How are you feeling?

> PAUL
> Um...not too bad.

She turns back. Paul's eyes drift down to admire her ass.

> JAN
> What did the doctor say?

No response. He's too busy staring. She turns again -- he
glances hastily up.

> PAUL
> Oh, you know doctors. Gobble-de-
> gook, mostly.

She turns back, keeps working. He crosses the room, eyeing her
ass all the way...and surprises her by pressing up against her
from behind, running his hands along her hips.

> JAN
> Paul? What are you doing?

He starts laying kisses on the back of her neck, giving her
pleasant shivers, murmuring:

> PAUL
> What's it feel like?

(CONTINUED)

> JAN
> I know what it <u>feels</u> like...it
> feels great...but...Paul...

He's getting her breathless. She turns into his arms and they get into some passionate kissing. It's not long before they're frantically peeling each other's clothes off...

INT - BEDROOM - NIGHT

...and we find them having a wild tumble in the sheets, both moaning and groaning, sweating and panting. She pushes him flat on the bed, pauses to catch her breath...

> JAN
> Those must've been some pills.

...and they keep going, rutting like crazed weasels...

EXT - HOUSE - NIGHT

...as their moans go drifting into the night...

> FADE TO:

SAME ANGLE AS ABOVE - DAWN

...and they're <u>still</u> moaning up there as the sun creeps up.

INT - BEDROOM - MORNING

Jan lies exhausted after the latest go-round. She catches her breath, looks over at Paul.

> JAN
> Paul? Not that I'm complaining.
> But we haven't gone four times in
> one night since we were nineteen.
>   (off his look)
> Wanna tell me what's going on?

> PAUL
> Well...thing is...I never actually
> got to the doctor yesterday...

She gives him a look -- oh?

> CUT TO:

INT - LIVING ROOM - MORNING

Paul is on the phone:

THE
GREEN
MILE

(CONTINUED)

                    PAUL
          Brutal? Listen...I'm thinking of
          taking the morning off sick. You
          cover the fort for me?
                    (beat)
          That's swell. Thanks. Yeah, I'm
          sure I'll feel better. Okay.

He hangs up, turns to Jan.

                    JAN
          You sure you ought to do this?

                    PAUL
          I'm not sure what I'm sure of.

                                        CUT TO:

EXT - ROAD TO TEFTON - DAY

Paul's Model T comes putt-putting up the road past a sign that
reads: "Trapingus County Welcomes You." Below it is nailed an
addendum crudely painted by hand: "No Jobs Here! Transients
Turn Back!"

EXT - HOUSE IN TEFTON - DAY

Paul pulls up, exits the car. CYNTHIA HAMMERSMITH, a careworn
young woman, appears at the screen door and peers out.

                    PAUL
          Ma'am? Have I found the
          Hammersmith residence?

EXT - BACK PORCH - DAY

BURT HAMMERSMITH, public defender for Trapingus County, sits
with a cold soda and a magazine, watching his TWO CHILDREN
playing on a swing at the far end of the backyard. The screen
door opens as Cynthia ushers Paul out.

                    CYNTHIA
          I offer you a cold drink?

                    PAUL
          Yes, ma'am, a cold drink would be
          fine. Thank you.

She goes back inside. Burt rises.

                    PAUL
          Mr. Hammersmith. Your office said
          I might find you at home today. I
          hope I'm not troubling you.

THE
GREEN
MILE
54

                                        (CONTINUED)

                         BURT
               That depends, Mr.--?

                         PAUL
               Paul Edgecomb. I'm the E Block
               superintendent at Cold Mountain.

                         BURT
               The Green Mile. I've heard of it.
               Lost a few clients your way.

                         PAUL
               That's why I'm here. I'd like to
               ask you about one of them.

Burt settles back down, motions "please sit."

                         BURT
               Which client? Now you got my
               curiosity aroused.

                         PAUL
               John Coffey.

                         BURT
               Ah, Coffey. He causing you
               problems?

                         PAUL
               No, can't say he is. He doesn't
               like the dark. He cries on
               occasion. Other than that...

                         BURT
               Cries, does he? Well, he's got a
               lot to cry about, I'd say. You
               know what he did.

                         PAUL
                    (nods)
               I read the court transcripts.

Cynthia reappears, hands Paul a cold lemonade.

                         PAUL
               Thank you, Missus.

                         CYNTHIA
               My pleasure. Kids! Lunch is about
               ready! Y'all come on up!

She goes back inside, but the kids aren't quite able to tear
themselves away from their play.

THE
GREEN
MILE

55

(CONTINUED)

                    BURT
          What exactly are you trying to
          find out? Satisfy my curiosity,
          I'll see if I can satisfy yours.

                    PAUL
          I've wondered if he ever did
          anything like that before.

                    BURT
          Why? Has he said anything?

                    PAUL
          No. But a man who does a thing
          like that has often developed a
          taste for it over time. Occurred
          to me it might be easy enough to
          follow his backtrail and find out.
          A man his size, and colored to
          boot, can't be that hard to trace.

                    BURT
          You'd think so, but you'd be
          wrong. Believe me, we tried. It's
          like he dropped out of the sky.

                    PAUL
          How can that be?

                    BURT
          We're in a Depression. A third of
          the country's out of work. People
          are drifting by the thousands,
          looking for jobs, looking for that
          greener grass. Even a giant like
          Coffey wouldn't get noticed
          everywhere he goes...not until he
          kills a couple of little girls.

                    PAUL
          He's...strange, I admit. But there
          doesn't seem to be any real
          violence in him. I know violent
          men, Mr. Hammersmith. I deal with
          'em day in and day out.

     Burt smiles, realizing:

                    BURT
          You didn't come up here to ask me
          whether he might have killed
          before. You came up here to see if
          I think he did it at all. That's
          it, isn't it?

                                        (CONTINUED)

                    PAUL
          Do you?

                    BURT
          One seldom sees a less ambiguous
          case. He was found with the
          victims in his arms. Blurted out a
          confession right then and there.

                    PAUL
          Yet you defended him.

                    BURT
          Everyone is entitled to a defense.

Cynthia hollers from an open window:

                    CYNTHIA
          Kids! Lunch!

                    BURT
          Y'all listen to your Momma, now!

The kids start this way. Burt turns back to Paul.

                    BURT
          Tell you something. You listen
          close, too, because it might be
          something you need to know.

                    PAUL
          I'm listening.

                    BURT
          We had us a dog. No particular
          breed, but gentle. Ready to lick
          your hand or fetch a stick. Just a
          sweet mongrel, you know the kind.
                    (Paul nods)
          In many ways, a good mongrel dog
          is like your negro. You get to
          know it, and often you get to love
          it. It is of no particular use,
          but you keep it around because you
          think it loves you. If you're
          lucky, Mr. Edgecomb, you never
          have to find out any different. My
          wife and I were not so lucky.
          Caleb. Come here for a second.

The little boy comes to him, staring at his feet. Burt tries
to raise the boy's chin. The boy resists for a moment...

                    BURT
          Please, son.

                                        (CONTINUED)

...and then his face comes around. He's horribly scarred on that side, the eye missing.

> BURT
> He has the one eye. I suppose he's
> lucky not to be blind. We get down
> on our knees and thank God for
> that much, at least. Right Caleb?
> (the boy nods shyly)
> Okay, go on in now.

The boy races inside after his sister. Paul follows Burt's gaze off toward the rear of the property, where an unoccupied doghouse stands weathered and sad in the weeds.

> BURT
> That dog attacked my boy for no
> reason. Just got it in his mind
> one day. Same with John Coffey. He
> was sorry afterwards, of that I
> have no doubt...but those little
> girls stayed raped and murdered
> nonetheless. Maybe he'd never done
> it before -- my dog never bit
> before, but I didn't concern
> myself with that. I went out there
> with my rifle and grabbed his
> collar and blew his brains out.

> PAUL
> I'm sorry for your trouble.

Burt acknowledges the condolence with a gracious nod.

> BURT
> I'm as enlightened as the next
> man, Mr. Edgecomb. I would not
> bring slavery back for all the tea
> in China. I believe we have to be
> humane and generous in our efforts
> to solve the race problem. But we
> have to remember that the negro
> will bite if he gets the chance,
> just like a mongrel dog will bite
> if it crosses its mind to do so.
> (beat)
> Is Coffey guilty? Yes, he is.
> Don't you doubt it, and don't you
> turn your back on him. You might
> get away with it once or even a
> hundred times...but in the end...

THE GREEN MILE

He raises his hand, makes biting motions with his fingers.

(CONTINUED)

                              BURT
                    You understand?

Paul says nothing. Burt gazes out again. Softly:

                              BURT
                    I'm gonna have to tear that old
                    doghouse down one of these days.

                                        CUT TO:

INT - PAUL'S MODEL T - DAY

Paul drives back to Cold Mountain, his heart conflicted...

INT - E BLOCK - DAY

...and he walks onto the Mile with a bundle wrapped in a dish
towel. Brutal glances up from the desk, sniffing the air.

                              PAUL
                    No, it's not for you.

Paul continues down the Mile. Whatever he's carrying, the
smell of it brings Del to his bars. Mr. Jingles comes
skittering out of his cigar box to join him.

                              DEL
                    Oh. Oh my.

Paul arrives at Coffey's cell. Coffey's on his bunk facing the
wall. His head comes around, drawn by the aroma. He sits up,
wipes the tears leaking from his eyes, looks at Paul.

                              COFFEY
                    I'm smelling me some cornbread.

Paul speaks softly so the others can't hear:

                              PAUL
                    It's from my missus. She wanted to
                    thank you.

Coffey nods thoughtfully, absorbing this notion. Then:

                              COFFEY
                    Thank me for what?

                              PAUL
                    You know. For helping me.

                              COFFEY
                    Helping you with what?

Paul motions discreetly to his crotch.

THE
GREEN
MILE

59

                                        (CONTINUED)

                    COFFEY
          Ohhh.
                    (beat)
          Was your missus pleased?

                    PAUL
          Several times.

Paul hands him the bundle through the bars. Coffey takes it,
uncovers the cornbread reverently, gazes back up.

                    COFFEY
          This all for me?

Paul nods. Across the way, Del watches longingly from the
bars. So does Mr. Jingles, perched near his foot.

                    DEL
          Oh my. John. I can smell it from
          here. I surely can.

                    COFFEY
                    (looks to Paul)
          Can I give some to Del?

                    PAUL
          It's yours, John. You do with it
          as you please.

John carefully scoops a big chunk of cornbread out with his
enormous hand, holds it through the bars to Paul.

                    COFFEY
          Here's for Del and Mr. Jingles then.

                    BILLY
          Hey! What about me? I'm'a get some
          too, ain't I?

Coffey looks to Paul -- do I have to?

                    PAUL
          It's yours, John. As you please.

                    COFFEY
          Well. Fine. I think I'll keep the
          rest, then.

He smiles like a big kid, digging in with his fingers. Paul
crosses the Mile to Del's cell, hands him his share.

                    PAUL
          Courtesy of the gentleman across
          the way.

                                        (CONTINUED)

                         DEL
          Oh, John. So very fine of you. So
          very kind. Mr. Jingles t'ank you.

                       COFFEE
                     (mouth full)
          ...wel'cm...

                        BILLY
          Hey! What about me? Don't you hold
          out on me, ya big dummy nigger!

Paul's temper flares -- he steps to Billy's cell.

                        PAUL
          You'll keep a civil tongue on my
          block.

Beat. Billy spits in Paul's face and follows it up with a big
grin -- what are you gonna do about that? Paul is seething as
he wipes the spit off, but keeps his temper where it belongs.

                        PAUL
          You get that one for free. But
          that's the last one.

Paul walks away. Billy laughs, hollering after him:

                        BILLY
          That's it? Just that little bitty
          one? Guess I'll have to pay out
          for the rest, huh?

                                        DISSOLVE TO:

INT - E BLOCK - DAY

Harry is walking the Mile, doing a cell check and jotting on a
clipboard. He pauses, making a notation...

...and a long stream of piss hits his leg. Billy's at his
bars, peeing on him. Harry jumps back, stunned. Billy howls
with laughter, hosing his aim wildly from side to side.

                        BILLY
          Yeehaaw! Good shot, weren't it?
          Oh, the look on your face!

Paul and Brutal come running. Harry's just flabbergasted:

                        HARRY
          You believe this? Son of a bitch
          pissed on me!

THE
GREEN
MILE
———
61

                                        (CONTINUED)

                    BILLY
          Hey, d'jall like that? I'm
          currently cooking some turds t'go
          with it! Nice soft ones! I'll have
          'em out t'yall tomorrow!

Paul stays calm, turns to Brutal, nods at the restraint room.

                    PAUL
          We've been looking to clear that
          room out anyway.

                                        TIMECUT:

A LINE OF GUARDS comes toting the last of the restraint room
stuff past Billy's cell while he heckles them from the bars...

                    BILLY
          Hey! Whassit now, movin' day?
          Y'all wanna come on in and dust a
          little? Y'can shine my knob for me
          while yer at it!

...and he pauses as Paul and Brutal step to the bars. Paul has
a canvas straitjacket. Brutal pulls his nightstick.

                    BILLY
          You can come in here on your legs,
          but you'll go out on your backs,
          Billy the Kid guarantee ya that.
                    (motions to Brutal)
          C'mon, fuckstick. No sneakin' up
          on me this time. We'll go man to
          man, see who's the better fel--

Brutal unlocks the cell -- and sidesteps, revealing Harry
pointing a fire hose. The hose erupts, driving Billy across
the cell with bone-jarring force. They batter him half-
senseless, then cut the water. Billy collapses in a heap.

Paul and Brutal drag him semi-conscious from his cell and
get the straitjacket on him. He comes around as they draw the
straps tight and pull him to his feet.

                    PAUL
          C'mon, Wild Bill. Little walky
          walky.

                    BILLY
          Don't you call me that! Wild Bill
          Hickok wasn't no range rider! He
          was just a bushwackin' John Law!
          Dumb sonofabitch sat with his back
          to the door and kilt by a drunk!

THE
GREEN
MILE

                                        (CONTINUED)

                    BRUTAL
          Oh, my suds and body! A <u>history</u>
          lesson! You just never know what
          you're gonna get when you come to
          work every day on the Green Mile.
          Thank you, <u>Wild</u> <u>Bill.</u>

Billy lets out a scream of rage and throws himself at Brutal.
Brutal, bored, shoves him back toward Paul, who then propels
him down the Mile toward the open restraint room door. Billy
sees where they intend to put him, resorts to pleading:

                    BILLY
          Oh, not in there! C'mon now, I'll
          be good! Honest Injun I will!
          No! No! Ummmmhhhh...urg...ah!

He suddenly drops to the floor, bucking and jerking wildly,
spewing drool. Harry's eyes go wide.

                    HARRY
          Holy Christ, he's pitchin' a fit!

Paul reaches down and unceremoniously starts dragging Billy
kicking and writhing the rest of the way.

                    PAUL
          He'll be fine, boys. Trust me on
          this one.

Brutal helps Paul toss Billy headlong into the padded room.
They slam the door...

RESTRAINT ROOM

...and Billy staggers to his feet in the straitjacket,
inarticulate with rage, starts throwing himself against the
door, screaming at the top of his lungs:

                    BILLY
          ALL I WANTED ME WAS A LITTLE
          CORNBREAD, YOU MOTHERFUCKERS!

                                        FADE TO:

INT - E BLOCK - NEXT DAY

Paul and Brutal unlock the restraint room. Billy looks up from
the corner, pale and drained. Softly:

                    BILLY
          I learnt my lesson. I'll be good.

                                        CUT TO:

INT - E BLOCK - DAY

Billy's back in his cell, quiet for a change. Toot-Toot is
outside the bars, mopping the floor. Billy notices a chocolate
Moon Pie in Toot's shirt pocket.

                    BILLY
          Pssss. Hey. Give'ya nickel for
          that Moon Pie.

Toot looks around. Nobody's watching, and a nickel's a nickel.
He steps to Billy's bars, swaps the Moon Pie for the money.

Toot hurries away. Billy unwraps the Moon Pie, makes sure he's
not being watched...and crams the entire thing in his mouth...

                                        DISSOLVE:

...and here comes Brutal strolling the Mile, doing a cell
check and jotting on a clipboard. He pauses, seeing:

Billy at his bars. Just standing there staring. His cheeks
bulging way out. Brutal steps closer, fascinated...what the
fuck is that? Billy waits until he's just a bit closer --

-- and he slams his fists against his own cheeks, propelling a
disgusting spew of liquefied chocolate sludge into Brutal's
face. Billy falls back onto his bunk, shrieking with laughter:

                    BILLY
          Li'l Black Sambo, yassuh, boss,
          yassuh, howdoo you do?

                    BRUTAL
               (beat, calmly)
          Hope your bags are packed.

                                        TIMECUT:

...and once again, Billy gets dragged to the restraint room,
kicking and screaming all the way. They toss him in, slam the
door. Brutal turns, still wiping traces of sludge off.

                    PAUL
          The Moon Pie thing was pretty
          original. Gotta give him that.

Brutal nods. They walk away as we

                                        FADE TO:

INT - E BLOCK - DAY

Paul and Brutal appear at Del's bars with Harry and Dean.

                                        (CONTINUED)

                    PAUL
          Del, grab your things. Big day for
          you and Mr. Jingles.

                    DEL
          Whatchoo talkin' bout?

                    BRUTAL
          Important folks heard about your
          mouse, wanna see him perform.

                    PAUL
          Not just guards, either. One of
          them's a politician all the way
          from the state capital, I believe.

Del swells with pride upon hearing this. He scrounges up Mr.
Jingles' props, steps from his cell, looks to Harry and Dean.

                    DEL
          You fellas comin'?

                    HARRY
          We got other fish to fry just now,
          Del, but you knock 'em for a loop.

Del nods happily, looks to Coffey in his cell.

                    COFFEY
          You knock 'em for a loop like Mr.
          Harry says, Del.

Brutal leads Del up the Mile, Paul and the others at their
heels. Percy's at the duty desk. He smirks and rolls his eyes
as Del goes by. The moment Brutal and Del are out the door...

                    PAUL
          Let's move along briskly, folks.
          There's not much time.

...Toot emerges from Paul's office where he's been hiding.

                    TOOT
          I'm sittin' down, I'm sittin'
          down, I'm sittin' down...

INT - OFFICE/ADMINISTRATION BUILDING - DAY

A HALF DOZEN GUARDS are waiting. We find Bill Dodge fixing the
tie of a fat good ol' boy named EARL.

                    EARL
          Been sweepin' floors here ten
          years, never had to wear no damn
          tie before.

THE
GREEN
MILE

65

(CONTINUED)

                         BILL
              You're a V.I.P. today, Earl, so
              just shut up.

A KNOCK at the door. Everybody takes a seat. Del is ushered
in by Brutal. Del faces his audience, puts his hands to his
chest in a "thank you" gesture worthy of Lillie Langtry before
her adoring public, then announces grandly:

                         DEL
              Messieurs et mesdames! Bienvenue
              au cirque de mousie!

INT - EXECUTION CHAMBER - DAY

The steel cap is lowered over Toot's head, the straps
tightened. TILT UP to Percy as:

                         PERCY
              Roll on two.

Behind his partition, Van Hay mimes flipping the switch.

                         VAN HAY
              That's that.

A pause. Percy looks anxiously to Paul, who's trading glances
with the other guards. Finally:

                         PAUL
              Very good. Very professional.

Percy smiles. Harry and Dean step up, slapping his back and
shaking his hand...

INT - E BLOCK - DAY

...and they're still chatting a short time later, waiting for
Del's return. Percy actually looks happy for a change, feeling
genuinely accepted for the first time...

Billy is watching from his cell. Just watching.

The door opens. Del returns with Mr. Jingles on his shoulder,
escorted by Brutal. Brutal is toting the cigar box and spool
like a magician's assistant carrying the boss' props.

                         DEL
              They love Mr. Jingles! They laugh
              and cheer and clap they hands!

                         PERCY
              Well, that's just aces. Pop back
              in your cell, old-timer.

(CONTINUED)

The generosity of Percy's tone catches Del completely off
guard. Del gives him a look of almost comical mistrust...

...and the old Percy comes back. He bares his teeth in a mock
snarl and curls his fingers as if to grab Del. It's a joke,
but Del doesn't know that -- he jerks back in fear and trips
over Brutal's big feet. Del goes down hard, hitting the
linoleum with the back of his head. Mr. Jingles jumps clear,
goes squeaking down the Mile. Del sits up, painfully clutching
his head. Brutal helps him up...

> BRUTAL
> Percy, you shit.

...and moves him toward his cell. Percy is actually moved to
apologize -- he starts after them with a half-laugh, drifting
much too close to Wild Bill's side of the Mile...

> PERCY
> Del! Hey, you numb wit, I didn't
> mean nothin' by it! You all ri--

...and Wild Bill's arms thrust out, grabbing Percy and slamming
him back against the bars with an arm around his throat. Percy
squeals like a pig in a slaughter-chute, thinking he's gonna
die. The guards scramble, drawing their clubs -- as Billy
strokes Percy's hair and whispers in his ear:

> BILLY
> Ain't you sweet. Soft. Like a
> girl. I druther fuck your asshole
> than your sister's pussy, I think.

Billy kisses Percy's ear -- and his hand drops down to squeeze
Percy's crotch. Paul pulls his sidearm, taking aim...

> PAUL
> Wharton!

...and Billy lets go, stepping back with his hands raised,
laughing. Percy darts across the Mile in terror and cringes
against the cell opposite, breathing so loud and fast it
almost sounds like sobbing.

> BILLY
> I let 'im go, I'us just playin'
> and I let 'im go! Never hurt a
> hair on his purty head!
> > (grins at Percy)
> Your noodle ain't limp at all,
> loverboy! I think you sweet on ol'
> Billy the Kid...
> > (sniffs his fingers)
> ...oooh, but smell you.

THE
GREEN
MILE

Down at his cell, Del starts laughing shrilly. Everybody else starts to realize why, including Percy himself...<u>he looks down, sees the huge dark stain spreading at his crotch.</u>

>   DEL
>   Lookit, he done piss his pants!
>   Look what the big man done! He
>   bus' other people wid 'is stick,
>   *mais oui* some *mauvais homme,* but
>   someone touch him, he make water
>   in his pants jus' like a baby!

Percy just stares. Brutal shoves Delacroix into his cell.

>   BRUTAL
>   Learn when to shut up, Del.

Paul steps to Percy, puts a hand on his shoulder. Percy shakes his hand off, looks around at their faces, whispers:

>   PERCY
>   You talk about this to anyone,
>   I'll get you all fired. I swear
>   that to God.

>   PAUL
>   What happens on the Mile, stays on
>   the Mile. Always has.

The men nod solemnly. Nobody's going to talk about this. Percy looks at Delacroix still snorting in his cell, points at him.

>   PERCY
>   You keep laughing, you French-
>   fried faggot. You just keep
>   laughing.

Del falls silent. Percy turns and storms away as we

>   FADE TO BLACK

IN BLACKNESS, A TITLE CARD APPEARS:

>   **"The Bad Death of Eduard Delacroix"**

>   CUT TO:

INT - DEL'S CELL - DAY

Paul is sitting with Delacroix. Brutal is leaning against the bars. Del is throwing the spool. Mr. Jingles is fetching it.

The silence is thick. Just the clack-clatter of the spool, and the skitter-skitter of tiny mouse paws on concrete. It's getting on Paul's nerves in a big way. Softly:

>   (CONTINUED)

                    PAUL
        What about Dean? He's got a little
        boy would love a pet mouse, I bet.

Del looks horrified at the thought.

                    DEL
        How could a boy be trust wid Mr.
        Jingles? Maybe forget to feed him.
        And how he keep up wid his trainin',
        just a boy, *n'est-ce pas?*

Del tosses the spool again -- clack-clatter, skitter-skitter.

                    PAUL
        All right, I'll take him.

                    DEL
        T'ank you kindly, *merci beaucoup,*
        but you live out in the woods, and
        Mr. Jingles, he be scared to live
        out *dans la foret.*

                    PAUL
        He whisper that in your ear?

Del nods, tosses the spool again -- clack-clatter, skitter
skitter. Paul is completely out of ideas. But then:

                    BRUTAL
        How about Mouseville?

                    DEL
        Mouseville?

                    BRUTAL
        Tourist attraction down in
        Florida. Tallahassee, I think. Is
        that right, Paul? Tallahassee?

                    PAUL
              (level)
        Yeah, that's right. Tallahassee.
        Just down the road apiece from the
        dog university.

Brutal's mouth twitches, but he manages to keep a straight
face. He gives Paul a look -- don't blow this.

                    BRUTAL
        You think they'd take Mr. Jingles?
        You think he's got the stuff?

                    PAUL
        Might. He's pretty smart.

THE
GREEN
MILE

                     DEL
        Hey! What dis Mouseville?

                  BRUTAL
        Tourist attraction, I said. They
        got this big tent you go into--

                     DEL
        Like a *cirque?* You have to pay?

                  BRUTAL
        You shittin' me? Course you pay.
        Dime a piece, two cents for the
        kids. And inside the tent there's
        this mouse city made out of boxes
        and toilet paper rolls, with little
        windows so you can look in...

Percy is drifting up the block, listening too, but nobody's
really paying him much mind.

                  BRUTAL
        ...plus they got the Mouseville
        All-Star Circus. There's mice that
        swing on trapeze, mice that roll
        barrels, mice that stack coins...

                     DEL
        Dat's it! Dat's da place for Mr.
        Jingles! You gonna be a circus
        mouse after all! Gonna live in a
        mouse city down in Florida!

Del tosses the spool extra hard -- it takes a bad bounce off
the wall and goes clattering through the bars onto the Mile.
The mouse goes after it like a shot, too intent to notice:

<u>His</u> <u>old</u> <u>enemy</u> <u>Percy.</u>

                  BRUTAL
        Percy, no!

<u>Percy</u> <u>stomps</u> <u>the</u> <u>heel</u> <u>of</u> <u>his</u> <u>heavy</u> <u>work</u> <u>shoe</u> <u>down</u> <u>on</u> <u>Mr.</u>
<u>Jingles.</u> There's a SOFT SNAP as the mouse's back breaks.

Del screams in horror and throws himself at the bars, sobbing
the mouse's name. Percy looks to Brutal and Paul, smiles.

                  PERCY
        Knew I'd get him sooner or later.
        Just a matter of time, really.

He turns and strolls up the Mile, leaving Mr. Jingles dying in
a tiny pool of blood. Up at the duty desk, Dean and Harry get
up from a cribbage game, stunned and furious.

                                        (CONTINUED)

Percy strolls past, exits to the execution chamber. Del is
still screaming, all his pent-up terror and grief pouring out
at the dying mouse. And then comes a soft, urgent voice:

> COFFEY
> Give'm to me.

They turn. Coffey's got his arms out through his bars, one
massive hand spread open.

> COFFEY
> Give'm to me. Might still be time.

Paul hesitates, scoops the mouse up off the floor, wincing at
the feel of it. Splintered bones are poking at the hide.

> BRUTAL
> What are you doing?

Paul doesn't answer, just lays Mr. Jingles into Coffey's hand.
Coffey pulls the mouse in through his bars and lays his other
hand gently over it, cupping the creature. All we see now is
the tail hanging out the side, twitching weakly.

> BRUTAL
> Paul, what the hell--

Paul motions him quiet. Del is pleading softly at his bars:

> DEL
> Please, John. Oh Johnny, help him,
> please help him, *s'il vous plaît.*

Harry and Dean join the group. Everybody watching now.

Coffey puts his mouth to his cupped hands, inhales sharply.
The world hangs suspended for a moment. Coffey raises his
face, contorting as if desperately ill, starts making those
horrendous choking sounds in his throat...

> BRUTAL
> (softly)
> Oh, dear Jesus. The tail. Look at
> the tail.

They do. The tail is no longer weak and dying. It's snapping
briskly back and forth, as if ready to play.

Coffey makes that retching/gagging sound...and again exhales a
cloud of swirling black "insects" from his nose and mouth. The
men watch, speechless, as the "bugs" turn white and disappear.

Coffey bends down, opens his hand. Mr. Jingles bounds off his
fingers through the bars, racing past the guards' feet. They

(CONTINUED)

turn to see Del gather the mouse up, laughing and crying. Dean turns back to Coffey with a stunned whisper:

                    DEAN
          What did you do?

                    COFFEY
          I helped Del's mouse. He a circus
          mouse. Goan live in a mouse city
          down in...down in...

                    BRUTAL
               (numb)
          Florida?

Coffey nods, remembering.

                    COFFEY
          Boss Percy's bad. He mean. He step
          on Del's mouse.
               (softly)
          I took it back, though.

And with that, he lies back on his bunk and faces the wall. The others look to Paul, don't even know what to say.

                    PAUL
          Brute, come along with me.
               (to Harry and Dean)
          You fellas go on back to your
          cribbage game.

Harry nods numbly. Paul leads Brutal up the Mile...

EXECUTION CHAMBER

...and they enter to find Percy polishing Old Sparky's arms.

                    PERCY
          Don't start in on me. It was just
          a mouse. Never belonged here in
          the first place.

                    PAUL
          The mouse is fine. Just fine.
          You're no better at mouse-killing
          than anything else around here.

                    PERCY
          You expect me to believe that? I
          heard the goddamn thing crunch.

Paul steps closer, angry as we've ever seen him:

                                        (CONTINUED)

                PAUL
        Aren't you glad Mr. Jingles is
        okay? After all our talks about
        how we should keep the prisoners
        calm? Aren't you relieved?

                PERCY
        What kind of game is this?

                PAUL
        No game. See for yourself.

Beat. Percy stalks past them, heads out onto the Mile. Paul
and Brutal just wait, saying nothing. Brutal picks up the rag
left by Percy, resumes polishing chores on Old Sparky. Paul
stretches, cracks his neck. The silence heavy...

...until Percy reappears:

                PERCY
        You switched them! You switched
        them somehow, you bastards!

                BRUTAL
        I always keep a spare mouse in my
        wallet for occasions such as this.

                PERCY
        You're playing with me, the both
        of you! Just who the hell do you
        think you are--

Brutal grabs him, forces him bodily into the electric chair.
Paul bends close, getting right in Percy's face.

                PAUL
        We're the people you work with, Percy,
        but not for long. I want your word.

                PERCY
        My word?

                PAUL
        I put you out front for Del, you
        put in your transfer to Briar
        Ridge the very next day.

                PERCY
        What if I just call up certain
        people and tell them you're
        harassing me? Bullying me?

                PAUL
        Go ahead. I promise you'll leave
        your share of blood on the floor.

THE
GREEN
MILE

(CONTINUED)

                         PERCY
               Over a mouse? You think anyone's
               gonna give two shits?

                         PAUL
               No. But four men will swear you
               stood by while Wild Bill tried to
               strangle Dean to death. About that
               people will care, Percy. Even your
               uncle the governor will care.

                         BRUTAL
               Thing like that goes in your work
               record. Work record can follow a
               man around a long, long time.

Percy looks from one man to another, knowing he's trapped.

                         PAUL
               I put you out front, you put in
               your transfer. That's the deal.

Percy thinks it over, nods. He tries to get up, but Paul keeps
him pinned...and pointedly offers his hand.

                         PAUL
               You make a promise to a man, you
               shake his hand.

Percy hesitates, shakes Paul's hand...

HIGH WIDE ANGLE OF EXECUTION CHAMBER

...and Paul pulls him out of the electric chair as we

                                   DISSOLVE TO:

SAME ANGLE AS ABOVE - NEXT NIGHT

Witnesses are trickling in, filling the seats. A storm is
brewing, sending FLASHES OF LIGHTNING across the floors.

INT - DEL'S CELL - NIGHT

Del sits with Mr. Jingles in his lap, stroking the mouse
between the ears. Paul, Brutal, and Harry appear at the bars.

                         DEL
               Hey, boys. Say hi, Mr. Jingles.

                         PAUL
               Eduard Delacroix, will you step
               forward?

THE
GREEN
MILE

                                        (CONTINUED)

                    DEL
          Boss Edgecomb?

                    PAUL
          Yes, Del?

                    DEL
          Don' let nothin' happen to Mr.
          Jingles, okay?

Paul nods -- I promise. Del rises, steps to Paul.

                    DEL
          Here, take him.

Del lifts his hand. Mr. Jingles steps off onto Paul's shoulder
with no hesitation. Gently:

                    PAUL
          Del. I can't have a mouse on my
          shoulder while...you know.

                    COFFEY
          I'll take him, boss. Jus' for now.
          If Del don' mind.

                    DEL
          Yeah, you take 'im, John. Take him
          til' dis foolishment done -- *bien!*
                    (to Paul and Brutal)
          After, you take him down to
          Florida? To dat Mouseville?

                    BRUTAL
          We'll do it together, most likely.
          Maybe take a little vacation time.

Paul moves to Coffey's cell. The mouse skitters off Paul's
shoulder onto Coffey's hand.

                    DEL
          People pay a dime apiece to see
          him. Two cents for the kiddies.
          Ain't dat right, Boss Howell?

                    BRUTAL
          That's right, Del.

                    DEL
          You a good man, Boss Howell. You
          too, Boss Edgecomb. Wish I could'a
          met you bot' someplace else.

Del gives Mr. Jingles one last look, starts to cry.

THE
GREEN
MILE

                                        (CONTINUED)

                         DEL
              *Au revoir, mon ami. Je t'aime, mon
              petit.*

And they start to walk the Mile...

EXECUTION CHAMBER

Sweltering in the damp heat. Rain is pissing down, drumming
the tin roof. People glance up uneasily as THUNDER BOOMS. A
WOMAN is staring grimly at the electric chair.

                        WOMAN #1
              Hope he's good and scared. Hope
              he knows the fires are stoked, and
              that Satan himself is waiting.

ANGLE ON DOOR

Del enters, horrified to see Percy waiting at Old Sparky. Paul
gives Del's arm a reassuring squeeze, leads him forward...

IN A TIGHT SERIES OF SHOTS:

The clamps are applied. The straps drawn tight.

                        PERCY
              Roll on one.

The lights brighten on a RISING HUM. Witnesses look up.

ON THE MILE

Coffey looks up as the overheads flare hotter and hotter,
whispers to the mouse in his hands:

                        COFFEY
              You be still, Mr. Jingles. You be
              so quiet and so still.

RESUME EXECUTION CHAMBER

                        PERCY
              Eduard Delacroix, you have been
              condemned to die by a jury of your
              peers, sentence imposed by a judge
              in good standing in this state.
              You have anything to say before
              sentence is carried out?

Del tries to speak. Doesn't quite manage the first time. Licks
his lips and tries again.

(CONTINUED)

>   DEL
>   I sorry for what I do. I give
>   anything to take it back, but I
>   can't. God have mercy on me.
>   (whispers to Paul)
>   Don' forget 'bout Mouseville.

Paul and Brutal nod -- and are stunned as:

>   PERCY
>   No such place. That's just a fairy
>   tale these guys told you to keep
>   you quiet. Just thought you should
>   know, faggot.

The stricken look in Del's eyes tells us a part of him <u>had</u> known all along. Paul and Brutal would both like to deck Percy right about now, and he knows it -- he gives them a "what are you gonna do about it" smile.

Nothing they <u>can</u> do. Paul nods to Harry, who takes the black mask from the back of the chair and rolls it down over Del's head, leaving the top of his shaved head exposed.

PERCY

takes the sponge and bends down to the bucket of brine. The others don't see it, but <u>we</u> do:

<u>Percy only pretends to dip the sponge and soak it. It never touches the water.</u> He straightens up and places the sponge atop Delacroix's head, hiding it with his hands.

The cap is lowered. Paul and the others haven't yet realized what's happened. THUNDER BOOMS and LIGHTNING CRASHES as Percy hides a smile, steps back to address the condemned:

>   PERCY
>   Electricity shall now be passed
>   through your body until you are
>   dead, in accordance with state
>   law. God have mercy on your soul.

TIGHT ON PAUL

as realization starts to dawn. He stares at the bucket, then across the floor to Delacroix, coming to terms with the evidence of his eyes -- <u>there's no water on the floor or dripping down the sides of Del's neck.</u>

Paul's eyes widen. A stunned beat of horror. He starts to open his mouth to scream "NO!," but Percy beats him to it with:

>   PERCY
>   Roll on two.

THE
GREEN
MILE

(CONTINUED)

Van Hay flicks the switch. <u>WHAM!</u> The electricity hits home and
Del rocks forward, riding the current.

Then things start to go horribly wrong.

The HUMMING loses its steadiness and starts to waver with a
CRACKLING SOUND. Tendrils of smoke begin curling from under
the cap, a mixture of burning hair and sponge. Brutal shoots
Paul a horrified look. Paul responds with a harsh whisper:

> PAUL
> Sponge is dry!

Delacroix begins twisting and jittering in the chair, his
masked face snapping violently from side to side, his legs
pistoning up and down in his restraints.

There's a MUFFLED POP from under the cap, like a pine knot
exploding in a hot fire. Smoke starts coming through the
fabric of the mask, puffing upward. Del is being cooked alive.
Paul spins to the partition, hollering --

> PAUL
> JACK!

-- but Brutal grabs his arm, whispers fiercely:

> BRUTAL
> Don't you tell him to stop. Don't
> you do it. It's too late for that.

Paul turns back, helpless. The other guards are trading wild
looks, unable to believe what's happening. Even Percy looks
aghast -- he was expecting something, but not this.

Del begins SCREAMING -- the wild, hysterical sound of an
animal being shredded alive in a hay baler. The HUMMING goes
uneven and ragged, the lights rising and falling...

ON THE MILE

...as Del's screams rise and fall with them, echoing up the
corridor.

COFFEY'S CELL

Coffey's shaking and screaming too, feeling Del's pain, arms
quaking against invisible clamps, head jerking violently. An
involuntary <u>muscle</u> <u>spasm/white</u> <u>flash</u> zaps Mr. Jingles clean
out of his hand. The mouse shoots through the bars onto the
Mile, skidding across the linoleum, squealing in pain and
terror down toward the restraint room door...

(CONTINUED)

BILLY'S CELL

Wild Bill's having the time of his life, swinging on his bars like a monkey in a cage, howling at the top of his lungs:

                    BILLY
          HE'S COOKIN' NOW! THEY COOKIN' HIM
          GOOD! NEAR ABOUT DONE, I RECKON!

RESUME EXECUTION CHAMBER

Wrong. Del's nowhere <u>near</u> about done. He's slamming back and forth in the chair hard enough to shake the platform, twisting hard against the leather restraints. We hear BONES BREAKING. A WOMAN SCREAMS. Witnesses start rising to their feet:

                    WITNESSES
          What the hell's happening to
          him?...Are those clamps going to
          hold?...Christ, the <u>smell!</u>...Is
          this normal?

<u>The mask bursts into flame on Delacroix's face.</u> Van Hay hollers through the wire mesh, horrified:

                    VAN HAY
          SHOULD I KILL THE JUICE?

                    PAUL
          NO! ROLL, FOR CHRIST'S SAKE, ROLL!

Harry scoops up the bucket of water to throw it.

                    PAUL
          No water! No water! You crazy?

Harry backs off with a look of dazed understanding -- you don't throw water on a man getting juiced. Right. He drops the bucket, races to get the chemical fire extinguisher instead.

The flaming mask peels away, revealing Del's charring face. His eyeballs are misshapen globs of burning white jelly blown out of their sockets. The ATTENDING DOCTOR faints dead away.

Pandemonium now in the room. People shouting and hurrying for the exit, chairs falling over, women screaming:

                    WOMAN #1
          Stop it, stop it, oh can't you see
          he's had enough?

Hal grabs Paul by the shoulder, spins him around.

                    HAL
          Why don't you shut it down?

THE
GREEN
MILE

79

                                        (CONTINUED)

                              PAUL
                    He's still alive! You want me to
                    shut down while he's still alive?

Hal is horrified at the thought. Del is jittering and
screaming, rocking from side to side, smoke pouring from his
nostrils and mouth, his tongue sizzling purple-black.

The witnesses are crowding and shoving to get out, but the
back door is locked. All they can do is cluster there.

Paul sees Percy with his head turned away. He grabs him,
forces his head around.

                              PAUL
                    You <u>watch,</u> you son of a bitch!

Harry steps up, the extinguisher in his hands. Waiting. Del
finally slumps over. He's still vibrating, but now it's just
the effect of current flowing through his body.

                              PAUL
                        Kill it!

Van Hay kills the current. The HUMMING DIES. Brutal grabs the
extinguisher from Harry, shoves it into Percy's hands.

                             BRUTAL
                    You do it. You're running the
                    show, ain't you?

Percy, sick and dazed, aims the extinguisher and hoses the
smoking corpse. Hal is near the back, calming the crowd:

                              HAL
                    It's all right, folks, it's all
                    under control. Just a power surge
                    from the storm, that's all,
                    nothing to worry about...

                              PAUL
                    Dean, get doc's stethoscope.

Dean drops to the doctor's bag, digs through it, hands up the
stethoscope. Paul plugs them into his ears. People are moaning
and sobbing at the back of the room:

                              MAN
                    Oh my God! Is it always like this?

                            WOMAN #2
                    Why didn't somebody tell me? I
                    never would have come!

(CONTINUED)

Paul wipes some foam away from Delacroix's chest, places the stethoscope pad to the raw flesh, and nods to Brutal -- it's over.

                              CUT TO:

INT - ACCESS TUNNEL - NIGHT

Paul and the others bring the stretcher down, lay the corpse on the gurney. Percy starts stammering excuses:

                         PERCY
              I didn't know the sponge was
              supposed to be wet--

Brutal hauls off and slugs him. A scuffle ensues as the others grab Brutal and pull him off.

                         PAUL
              Brutal, no!

                         BRUTAL
              What do you mean, no? How can you
              say no? You saw what he did!

                         PAUL
              Delacroix's dead, nothing can
              change that, and Percy's not worth
              it!

                         BRUTAL
              So he just gets away with it? Is
              that how it works?

Hal comes lunging down the stairs, furious:

                         HAL
              What the fuck was that? Jesus
              Christ, three witnesses puked all
              over the floor up there! And the
              smell! I got Van Hay to open both
              doors, but that smell won't come
              out for five damn years, that's
              what I'm betting! And that asshole
              Wharton is singing about it! I can
              hear him!

                         PAUL
                    (quietly)
              Can he carry a tune, Hal?

This pulls the plug on the moment -- Hal snorts, triggering laughter among the men, a wild release of tension and fear. Everybody starts feeling a bit saner again as it dies down:

81

                                        (CONTINUED)

                         HAL
              Okay, boys. Okay. Now what the
              hell happened?

All eyes go to Percy. Hal turns, sees Percy's bloody lip.

                         HAL
              Percy? Something to say?

                         PERCY
              I didn't know the sponge was
              supposed to be wet.

Beat. A look of utter contempt from Hal.

                         HAL
              How many years you spend pissing
              on the toilet seat before somebody
              told you to put it up?

                         PAUL
              Percy fucked up, Hal. Pure and
              simple.

                         HAL
              Is that your official position?

                         PAUL
              Don't you think it should be?

Hal considers it, nods.

                         PAUL
              He'll be putting in a transfer
              request to Briar Ridge tomorrow.
              Moving on to bigger and better
              things. Isn't that right, Percy?

Percy nods. Hal steps close, gives him a tight, icy smile.

                         HAL
              You're a little asshole, and I
              don't like you a bit.
                    (off Percy's look)
              Have that transfer request on my
              desk first thing.

Hal heads back up the stairs. Brutal shoves Percy aside and
wheels Delacroix's body down the tunnel.

INT - E BLOCK - NIGHT

Paul returns to find Wild Bill making up a song in his cell:

                                            (CONTINUED)

> BILLY
> (singing)
> Barbecue! Me and you! Stinky,
> pinky, phew-phew-phew! Weren't
> Billy or Jilly or Hilly or Roy --
> it was a French-fried faggot named
> Delacroix!

> PAUL
> You're about ten seconds away from
> spending the rest of your life in
> the padded room.

Billy falls silent. Paul continues down the Mile to Coffey's cell. Coffey's on his bunk, face streaked with tears. He wipes his eyes with the heels of his hands like an exhausted child.

> COFFEY
> Poor Del. Poor old Del.

> PAUL
> Yes. Poor old Del. John, are _you_
> okay?

> COFFEY
> I could feel it from here.

> PAUL
> What do you mean? You could _hear_
> it? Is that what you mean?

> COFFEY
> He out of it now, though. He the
> lucky one. No matter how it
> happened, Del the lucky one.

Paul realizes he won't get a coherent answer.

> PAUL
> Where's Mr. Jingles?

> COFFEY
> (points vaguely)
> Ran down there. Don't think he'll
> be back.
> (guilty whisper)
> He felt it too. Through me. Din'
> mean t'hurt him none. Couldn't
> help it. All that hurt jus' spill
> out.
> (beat)
> Awful tired now, boss. Dog tired.

Coffey lays down, turns to face the wall.

THE
GREEN
MILE

83

(CONTINUED)

                              PAUL
                    Me too, John. Me too.

                                        CUT TO:

INT - PAUL'S HOUSE - NIGHT

Paul enters in darkness, hangs his hat. He drifts into the
kitchen, clicks on the radio. SOFT MUSIC BEGINS: Gene Austin
singing "Did You Ever See A Dream Walking?"

He pours a drink at the kitchen table, takes a sip, lays the
glass down. Jan sleepily appears from the darkness behind him,
entering the kitchen. He realizes she's there, glances back.

She can sense the weight on his soul. She comes to him, folds
his head into her arms. They stand that way, he drawing
strength and she giving it, as the music plays on...

                                        DISSOLVE TO:

SEQUENCE WITH MUSIC:

INT - CHURCH - MORNING

CAMERA TRACKS the pews to find Paul and Jan seated together in
the congregation, voices raised in hymn...

EXT - COUNTRY ROAD - MORNING

Paul's Model T comes up the road. He and Jan are taking a
drive, still in their Sunday best...

EXT - HAL'S HOUSE - MORNING

The Model T rattles up the long, rutted driveway and comes to
a stop. Paul cuts the engine.

                              PAUL
                    I hate this.

                              JAN
                    I know.

Hal appears from the backyard, looking tired, gives them a
welcoming wave. Paul and Jan get out of the car...

EXT - BACKYARD - MORNING

...and follow Hal into the garden. MELINDA MOORES is sitting
in the sun, frail and wasted, a blanket on her knees. She'd be
beautiful if not for the cancer killing her.

Paul is shocked at her appearance, hides it as best he can.
Jan covers for him -- she drops to Melinda's side with a warm

                                        (CONTINUED)

smile and a kiss, takes the woman's frail hands in hers.

Paul catches Jan's eye. The look he gives her says it all -- I
don't know what I'd do without you...

                                        DISSOLVE:

...and we find Paul and Hal talking quietly over the barbecue
while the women visit b.g.:

                    PAUL
          How are you holding up?

                    HAL
          Well as I can.

A brief, loaded silence. Hal's being evasive. Softly:

                    PAUL
          Have you told her yet?

                    HAL
          Aw, Christ, Paul, how can I? I
          haven't accepted it myself yet.

                    PAUL
              (gently)
          I'm not judging.

Beat. Hal softens, grateful for that. He gazes toward Melinda.

                    HAL
          She's having one of her good days.
          I thank God for that.

                    PAUL
          What's a bad day?

                    HAL
          Sometimes she's...not herself
          anymore. She swears.

                    PAUL
          Swears?

                    HAL
          It just pops out, the most awful
          language you can imagine. She
          doesn't even know she's doing it.
          I didn't know she'd ever <u>heard</u>
          words like that...and to hear her
          say them in her sweet voice...
              (gazes off)
          I'm glad she's having a good day,
          Paul. I'm glad for you and Jan.

                                        (CONTINUED)

MELINDA AND JAN

Jan is carefully weaving a sprig of tiny wildflowers into Melinda's hair. Melinda raises her hand to her hair self-consciously. The hand trembles. Jan gives her a smile.

> JAN
> You're beautiful.

> MELINDA
> Am not.

> JAN
> Are too.

Jan finishes, leans back to judge her work, smiles. Melinda smiles too. They share an amiable silence, a rare moment of friendship and warmth. Softly:

> MELINDA
> You'll take care of him, won't
> you? After I'm gone? You'll look
> after Hal? You and Paul?

> JAN
> (beat)
> Of course we will.

Melinda smiles, reassured, brushes back a wisp of Jan's hair.

> MELINDA
> I'm glad.

> DISSOLVE TO:

INT - PAUL'S AND JAN'S BEDROOM - NIGHT

Paul is wide awake, staring at the dark. Jan can <u>sense</u> him brooding. She rolls over sleepily.

> JAN
> Honey? If you don't say what's on
> your mind, I'm afraid I'll have to
> smother you with a pillow.

> PAUL
> I'm thinking I love you. I'm
> thinking I don't know what I'd do
> if you were gone.

> JAN
> Oh.

(CONTINUED)

                    PAUL
               (beat)
     I'm also thinking I'd like to have
     the boys over tomorrow.

Off Jan's look, we

                              CUT TO:

EXT - PAUL AND JAN'S BACKYARD - DAY

A sun-dappled setting. Brutal, Harry, and Dean are seated at
an outdoor table with Paul and Jan. Serving plates are being
passed, everybody digging in:

                    THE MEN
               (various, ad-lib)
     Ma'am, you sure know how to fry up
     some fine chicken...Brutal, don't
     hog the taters now...Try that corn
     yet? It's something special...

Paul softly interjects:

                    PAUL
     You saw what he did with the mouse.

This stops everybody cold. Dean puts his chicken down, wipes
his hands. Looks are traded in the silence.

                    BRUTAL
     I could'a gone the rest of the day
     without you bringing that up.

                    DEAN
     I could'a gone the rest of the year.

                    PAUL
     He did it to me too. He put his
     hands on me and took my bladder
     infection away.

The men absorb this. Brutal glances to Jan.

                    JAN
     When he came home, he was...all
     better.

                    DEAN
     You're talking about an authentic
     healing. A praise-Jesus miracle.

                    PAUL
     I am.

THE
GREEN
MILE

87

                         (CONTINUED)

                         BRUTAL
               If you say it, I accept it. But
               what's it got to do with us?

Jan looks to Paul, realization starting to dawn:

                         JAN
               Melinda? Oh, Paul...

                         BRUTAL
               Melinda? Melinda Moores?

Paul nods -- that's who we're talking about.

                         JAN
               You really think you can help her?

                         PAUL
               It's not a bladder infection, or
               even a busted up mouse. But there
               might be a chance.

                         HARRY
               Hold on now. You're talking about
               our jobs. Sneak a sick woman onto
               a cellblock?

                         PAUL
               Hal would never allow that. You
               know him, he wouldn't believe
               something unless it fell on him.

                         BRUTAL
               So you're talking about taking
               John Coffey to her. That's more
               than just our jobs, Paul. That's
               prison time if we get caught.

                         DEAN
               Damn right it is.

                         PAUL
               Not you, Dean. Way I've got it
               figured, you'd stay on the Mile.
               Worse came to worse, you could
               deny everything.

Dean considers this, glances around the table.

                         DEAN
               Why do I have to stay behind?

                                        (CONTINUED)

PAUL
(takes Jan's hand)
Our boy's grown up, gone off to
school. Harry's kids are all
married. Brutal's a single man.
You're the only one here with two
youngsters, and a third on the
way.

DEAN
(beat)
Well...I suppose that's right.

HARRY
Let's not discuss this like we're
thinking of doing it. Brutal, help
me out here...

Brutal lets out a long breath, considering. He looks to Paul.

BRUTAL
I'm sure she's a fine woman...

JAN
The finest.

PAUL
What's happening to her is an
offense, Brutal. To the eyes and
the ears and the heart.

BRUTAL
I have no doubt. But we don't know
her like you and Jan do...do we?

PAUL
That's why it's a lot to ask.

HARRY
It is. Let's not forget Coffey's a
murderer. What if he escapes? I'd
hate losing my job or going to
prison, but I'd hate having the
death of a child on my conscience
even more.

PAUL
I don't think that'll happen...
(beat, softly)
...in fact, I don't think he did
it at all.

The men are stunned by this. Off their looks:

THE
GREEN
MILE

89

(CONTINUED)

                    PAUL
          I just can't see God putting a
          gift like that in the hands of a
          man who would kill a child.

                    HARRY
          Well, that's a tender notion, but
          the man's on death row for the
          crime. Plus he's huge. If he tried
          to get away, it'd take a lot of
          bullets to stop him.

                    BRUTAL
          We'd all have shotguns in addition
          to sidearms. I'd insist on that.
                    (to Paul)
          He tried anything, we'd have to
          take him down. You understand.

                    PAUL
          I understand.

                    BRUTAL
                    (beat)
          So. Tell us what you had in mind.

                                        FADE TO BLACK

IN BLACKNESS, A TITLE CARD APPEARS:

                    "Night Journey"

                                        CUT TO:

INT - INFIRMARY BUILDING/DISPENSARY - NIGHT

A FLASHLIGHT BEAM plays across a glass cabinet, scanning the
contents. The beam pauses. A hand enters frame, unlocks the
cabinet, pulls out a bottle of morphine tablets...

...and WE ANGLE TO Brutal as he shakes half a dozen pills onto
his palm, pockets them, replaces the bottle on the shelf. He
turns and slips a five dollar bill to a NIGHTSHIFT ORDERLY.

                    BRUTAL
          I was never here.

                    ORDERLY
          Shit, for five bucks, you was
          never nowhere.

                                        CUT TO:

INT - E BLOCK ACCESS TUNNEL - NIGHT

A MORPHINE PILL is being crushed to powder on the stainless
steel gurney. TILT UP to Paul crushing the pills. Brutal
carefully scrapes the powder onto a small sheet of paper...

INT - PAUL'S INNER OFFICE - NIGHT

Percy is parked in Paul's chair with his feet up, reading a
book titled: "CARING FOR MENTAL PATIENTS."

INT - E BLOCK - NIGHT

Harry and Dean are playing cards at the duty desk, tension
thick, cards slapping softly as the seconds tick by. Paul and
Brutal finally show up toting bottles of RC Cola:

                    BRUTAL
          Fellas thirsty? Fresh out of the
          icebox.

                    DEAN
          Oh, gee. That's swell. Thanks.

                    HARRY
          Yeah. Hot in here. Boy howdy.

They begin popping the caps off, swigging cola. The sound of
it brings Billy to his bars.

                    BILLY
          Hey. Hey, I'm'a get some too?

                    BRUTAL
          My ass you get some too.

                    PAUL
          You think you deserve any?

                    HARRY
               (checks a clipboard)
          Day report says he's been okay.

                    BILLY
          Hell, yes, I been behaved. C'mon,
          now, don't be stingy hogs.

Paul shrugs to Brutal -- why not? Brutal pops the top off a
bottle, passes it to Paul. Paul grabs a tin cup, sets it on
the desk...<u>and</u> <u>we</u> <u>see</u> <u>it</u> <u>contains</u> <u>the</u> <u>morphine</u> <u>powder.</u> He
pours the cola, swirls it around...

ANGLE THROUGH COFFEY'S BARS

...as Coffey looks up, sensing something happening. He peers

THE
GREEN
MILE

                                        (CONTINUED)

up the Mile as Paul walks to:

BILLY'S CELL

Billy reaches for the cup, but Paul keeps it out of reach.

> PAUL
> You gonna <u>stay</u> behaved?

> BILLY
> C'mon, you clunk, gimme that.

> PAUL
> You promise me, or I'll drink it
> myself right here in front of you.

> BILLY
> C'mon now, don't be that way. I
> be good.

Paul lets him take the cup. Billy knocks it back, draining it
in three huge swallows. He lets out an awesome belch.

> PAUL
> Cup.

> BILLY
> What if I decide to keep it?

> PAUL
> We'll break out the fire hose and
> take it anyway. And you will have
> drunk your last R.C. Cola. Unless
> they serve 'em down in hell.

Billy's smile fades. He hands the cup through the bars. Paul
takes it, turns and heads back to --

THE DUTY DESK

-- where Brutal, Harry, and Dean have been watching the entire
exchange with their hearts in their throats...

> DISSOLVE:

...and we find Billy staring glassy-eyed at the ceiling. He
keels over on his bunk. ANGLE TO Paul and Brutal stepping to
the bars with Harry and Dean.

> PAUL
> Anybody wants to back out, now's
> the time. After this, there's no
> turning back.
> (off their looks)
> So? We gonna do this?

(CONTINUED)

A voice comes softly from down the way:

> COFFEY
> Sure. I'd like to take a ride.

Their heads come slowly around, staring at Coffey in shock.

> BRUTAL
> (to Paul)
> Guess we're all in.

INT - PAUL'S OFFICE - NIGHT

Percy looks up from his book as the door opens. Paul enters
with Brutal and Harry, ominously hemming the desk.

> PERCY
> What is this?

Paul pulls the canvas straitjacket from behind his back.

> PAUL
> Payback.

Percy jumps up and tries for the execution chamber, but Harry
grabs him, spins him back. A wild scuffle ensues as:

> PERCY
> Let go of me! Let go!

> PAUL
> Settle down, Percy!

Percy tries to jerk away, crashes into the desk. The book he
was reading falls to the floor --

-- and a "Tijuana Bible" is revealed within the pages. It's a
pornographic cartoon book of the type popular in the '30s,
featuring crude drawings of famous cartoon characters or movie
stars engaged in outlandish sexual acts. This one has Olive
Oyl getting it doggy-style from Popeye. The word balloon over
his head features his famous laugh: "Uk-uk-uk-uk!"

> BRUTAL
> Ooooh, Poicy! What would your
> mother say?

> PERCY
> Let go, you ignoramus! I know
> people! Big people!

> PAUL
> So you've said. C'mon, stick out
> your arms like a good boy.

THE
GREEN
MILE

                    PERCY
          I won't. And you can't make me.

                    BRUTAL
          You're dead wrong about that, you
          know.

Brutal grabs Percy by the ears, twisting hard. Percy lets out
a shriek -- not just of pain, but a dismayed understanding
that he's not going to bluster his way out of this one.

                    BRUTAL
          You gonna put your arms up? I'll
          rip your ears off. Use 'em for
          tea caddies. You know I will.

                    PAUL
          The man's ripping your ears off,
          Percy. I'd do as he says.

Percy jerks his arms up before him. They get the straitjacket
on him within seconds, binding him tight. Percy turns to Paul
on the verge of tears. Softly:

                    PERCY
          Please, Paul. Don't put me in with
          Wild Bill. Please.

                    PAUL
          You would think that.

Paul gives him a hard, angry shove...

INT - E BLOCK - NIGHT

...and they bring him down the Mile. Dean rises at the duty
desk, playing his "part," feigning shock and surprise:

                    DEAN
          Hey! Don't you fellas think the
          joke's gone far enough?

                    BRUTAL
          You stay out of our way, Dean, if
          you know what's good for you!

Brutal follows this up with a big, goofy sneer. Dean very
nearly blows it by laughing, but manages to maintain.

Percy gets hustled down to the restraint room door. Brutal
confiscates his holster and baton.

                    BRUTAL
          You'll get 'em back, don't worry.

(CONTINUED)

>   PERCY
>   That's more than I can say about
>   your jobs! All your jobs! You
>   can't do this to me! You can't!

Paul steps forward with a roll of strapping tape.

>   PAUL
>   Let you in on a little secret. We
>   can and we are.

He slaps the tape over Percy's mouth and shoves him back into
the restraint room. Percy stands breathing heavily through his
nose, making muffled mmmmph-mmmmph! sounds under the tape.

>   PAUL
>   You're going to have a few hours
>   of quiet time now, so you can
>   reflect on what you did to Del.

>   BRUTAL
>   (grins)
>   If you get lonely, think about
>   Olive Oyl...
>   (thrusting his hips)
>   ...uk-uk-uk-uk!

And they slam the door, shutting Percy into darkness.

A WALL-MOUNTED GUN SAFE

is unlocked, shotguns pulled out. The men load up, heading
down the Mile as:

>   PAUL
>   Let's go through it again -- what
>   do you say if somebody comes by?

>   DEAN
>   Coffey got upset just after lights
>   out, so we put the coat on him and
>   locked him in the restraint room.
>   They hear any kicking or fussing in
>   there, they'll think it's him.

>   PAUL
>   What about me?

>   DEAN
>   You're over in Admin pulling Del's
>   file and, uh, going over the
>   witnesses, on account of how big a
>   screw up the execution was...

They come to Coffey's cell.

THE
GREEN
MILE

                         COFFEY
          We goan for the ride now?

                          PAUL
           That's right.

The cell is unlocked. Coffey emerges. Paul motions them along.

                         BRUTAL
           What about us, Dean?

                          DEAN
           You and Harry and Percy are all
           down in the laundry doing your
           wash...probably take ya'll a few
           hours 'fore you're back--

A skinny white arm suddenly shoots out from Wild Bill's cell
and grabs Coffey by the wrist. The men gasp, shocked to see
Billy on his feet, grinning and weaving like a punch-drunk.

Coffey's reaction is beyond simple surprise; he's actually
trembling at Billy's touch as if some electrical circuit were
engaged. His eyes are wide and horrified, as if he'd just put
his hand in a basket full of snakes. He tries to pull away,
but Billy has him tight, that mysterious circuit blazing.

                         BILLY
                   (slurring wildly)
           Where you fink you're goin'?

Coffey responds softly, with utmost horror:

                         COFFEY
           You're a bad man.

                         BILLY
           S'right, nigger. Bad as you'd want.

Paul plucks Billy's hand off Coffey's arm -- and Coffey
flinches back as the circuit is broken.

                         BILLY
           Whooeee. Whole room's spinning.
           Like I'm shit-ass drunk. I have me
           some shine or what?

He turns and staggers back to his bunk, muttering all the way:

                         BILLY
           Niggers oughtta have they own
           'lectric chair. White man oughtn't
           havta sit in no nigger 'lectric
           chair, nossir...

THE
GREEN
MILE

96

                                                  (CONTINUED)

He goes face-first onto his bunk. Coffey is still staring.

> COFFEY
> He's a bad man.

INT - EXECUTION CHAMBER - NIGHT

Coffey is brought in...and freezes in horror at the sight of
Old Sparky. A whisper:

> COFFEY
> They're still in there. Pieces of
> them, still in there. I hear them
> screaming.

All eyes go to electric chair. It sits shrouded in shadow like
an ominous throne. Never before has this place felt so haunted
to the men. It makes the hairs on the neck stand up.

> PAUL
> John, come along! Right now,
> y'hear? C'mon! Toward that door!

Coffey finally responds, pulling away.

EXT - PRISON WALL - NIGHT

A massive iron door SQUEALS open onto a little-used fenced
enclosure. Paul and the others bring Coffey up from the access
tunnel below. Coffey's breath catches as he gazes wondrously
up at the stars, pointing:

> COFFEY
> Look, boss! It's Cassie, the lady
> in the rocking chair!

> PAUL
> Shhh. John, you have to be quiet
> now.

> COFFEY
> (whispering)
> You see her? You see the lady?

> BRUTAL
> We see her, John.

Harry goes first, hugging the shadows as he pulls his keys to
unlock the gate...

WIDE SHOT OF PRISON

...while TOWER GUARDS huddle in their enclosures atop the
walls. An occasional SPOTLIGHT cuts the darkness. FIREFLIES
dance in the fields and trees as far as the eye can see.

(CONTINUED)

Four dark figures detach from the shadows, hurrying across the lonely country road into the fields on the far side...

EXT - WOODS - NIGHT

Coffey's hand scoops up some fallen leaves. TILT UP to his face as he crunches them under his nose, inhaling their smell.

He sees the guards throwing him anxious looks. He misreads this, holds out of hand so they can smell too. They do it, just to make him happy.

                    PAUL
          C'mon, big boy, keep moving.

A FEW FIREFLIES come winking through frame as the group presses on...

ANOTHER AREA/WOODS

The trees are growing sparser, opening onto fields. MORE FIREFLIES are flitting into view, trailing in their wake...

                    BRUTAL
          How far is it?

                    HARRY
          Just up ahead...

Harry brings them to a thicket of trees. They start removing branches and boughs, uncovering a battered old FARMALL TRUCK hidden in the brush.

The men pause. Even more fireflies are swirling around them now, growing in number. It's getting downright weird. Coffey laughs softly, drawing their attention. A childlike smile has utterly transformed his face. He raises his hand, letting a firefly weave playfully in and out of his fingers.

                    COFFEY
          Hey there, little firefly. Where's
          Mrs. Firefly this evening?

Another firefly joins the first, both now dancing and blinking around his fingers. Coffey laughs again.

                    COFFEY
          Oh, there you is. You come out to
          play too?

The men stand gaping. The fireflies are flitting to Coffey as if to a beacon. He waves his hands slowly, fireflies blinking and trailing from his fingertips like magic dust.

                                        (CONTINUED)

They begin orbiting his shiny bald head like tiny glowing
planets orbiting a sun, their light kicking a mellow sheen off
his ebony skin. Coffey's eyes meet Paul's.

                    PAUL
          They seem...drawn to you.

                    COFFEY
          I love 'em, is why. They don't
          think no hurtful thoughts. They's
          just happy to be. Happy little
          lightning bugs...

The men don't know whether to be enchanted or terrified. Harry
gives Paul a look -- can we go? Please?

                    PAUL
          C'mon, big boy. Upsy-daisy.

Coffey clambers up on the stakebed. Paul and Brutal join him.
Harry gets in behind the wheel, jabs the starter button...

ON THE STAKEBED

...while Coffey sits with his back to the cab.

                    PAUL
          John? Do you know where we're
          taking you?

                    COFFEY
          Help a lady?

                    PAUL
          That's right. Help a lady. But how
          do you know?

                    COFFEY
          Dunno. Tell the truth, boss, I
          don't know much'a anything. Never
          have.

The truck pulls out. Coffey waves as the fireflies get left
behind, dwindling away like stars.

                    COFFEY
          Bye, fireflies. Bye.

WIDE ANGLE OF COUNTRYSIDE

The truck rumbles from the fields onto a dirt road, countless
fireflies swirling in its wake...

                                        DISSOLVE TO:

THE
GREEN
MILE

EXT - MOORES HOUSE - NIGHT

The truck appears, rumbling toward the house. The world is isolated and still.

IN THE TRUCK CAB

Harry stops and cuts the engine, leaving the headlights on. Silence now, save for the trilling of crickets.

IN THE STAKEBED

Paul and Brutal both look terrified now that they're actually here. An urgent whisper:

> BRUTAL
> We can still turn back.

Paul hesitates, wanting to do just that, but:

> COFFEY
> Boss, look. Someone's up.

Lights are coming on inside the house. Coffey rises and steps down from the truck, pulling Paul along. Brutal follows them.

> BRUTAL
> This is a mistake. Christ, Paul,
> what were we thinking?

> PAUL
> Too late now. Harry, keep John
> here until we call you.

Paul and Brutal walk to the front door as the lights inside the house keep clicking on. The last one finally comes on over the stoop, the front door opens a crack...and the twin barrels of a shotgun poke out into the night.

> HAL
> Who the hell goes there at two-
> thirty in the goddamn morning?

> PAUL
> Hal, it's us! It's Paul and
> Brutal -- it's us!

The door swings wider, revealing Hal's face gaunt and haggard in the yellow porch light, stunned to see them:

> HAL
> Paul? What are you doing here at
> this hour? Jesus, it's not a
> lockdown, is it? Or a riot?

THE GREEN MILE

(CONTINUED)

                    PAUL
          Hal, God's sakes, take your finger
          off the trigger...

Hal <u>doesn't,</u> aiming past them at the truck in the yard.

                    HAL
          Are you hostages? Who's out there?
          Who's by that truck?

Coffey steps into the glare of headlights with Harry tugging
on his arm, trying to hold him back. Hal cocks both hammers.

                    HAL
          John Coffey! Halt! Halt right
          there or I shoot!

His aim wavers as a woman's voice comes from upstairs:

                    MELINDA (O.S.)
          Hal? Who are you talking to, you
          fuck?

A frozen moment. Hal mortified. Paul gives him a look -- is
that <u>Melinda?</u> Hal's shotgun shifts back to Coffey -- <u>but Paul</u>
<u>steps in front of the muzzle.</u>

                    PAUL
          No one's hurt. We're here to help.

                    HAL
          Help <u>what?</u> I don't understand. Is
          this a prison break?

                    PAUL
          I can't explain <u>what</u> it is. You
          just have to trust me.

Coffey comes up the steps, brushes Paul aside, stops before
the warden. Hal blinks, his thoughts suddenly fuzzy -- it's
that benign hypnotic effect Coffey has.

                    HAL
          What do you...want?

                    MELINDA (O.S.)
          Hal! Make them go away! No
          salesmen in the middle of the
          night! No Fuller brushes! No
          French knickers with come in the
          crotch! Tell them to take a flying
          fuck in a rolling d...d...

We hear the sound of a GLASS BREAKING, then she begins to sob.

                                        (CONTINUED)

                    COFFEY
                 (a whisper)
          Just to help. Just to help, boss,
          that's all.

                    HAL
          You can't. No one can.

Coffey pulls the shotgun gently from Hal's grasp, hands it to
Paul. Coffey moves past Hal into the house...

INT - HOUSE - NIGHT

...and comes up the hallway toward the stairs.

                    HAL
          Don't you go up there! Don't you
          do it!

                    COFFEY
          Boss, you just be quiet now and
          let me be.

Coffey mounts the stairs with the others at his heels, heading
up toward that quavering voice:

                    MELINDA (O.S.)
          Stay out of here! Whoever you are,
          just stay out! I'm not dressed for
          visitors!

INT - BEDROOM - NIGHT

Coffey enters, trailed by the others. Paul pauses, horrified:

The woman propped up in bed barely resembles Melinda Moores
anymore. Her livid skin hangs in a loose trail of wrinkles,
one corner of her mouth twisted. Yellowish bile stains her
chin and the front of her nightgown. Her hair has gone white
and straw-like, her eyes glowering at Coffey with lively,
irrational interest:

                    MELINDA
          So big! Pull down your pants,
          let's have a look...

Hal groans with despair. Coffey just stands for a moment,
watching her from a distance, then approaches the bed...

                    MELINDA
          Don't come near me, pigfucker.

...but as he draws closer, a change occurs. Her features
soften, her eyes become more sane and aware.

                                        (CONTINUED)

                    MELINDA
          Why do you have so many scars? Who
          hurt you so badly?

                    COFFEY
          Don't hardly remember, ma'am.

Coffey sits on the edge of the bed. The lights seem to flare
hotter and brighter. Tears are forming in Melinda's eyes.

                    MELINDA
          What's your name?

                    COFFEY
          John Coffey, ma'am. Like the
          drink, only not spelt the same.

She lays back, staring at him with shining fascination. The
world seems to be slowing down, growing very still indeed...

...and he starts bending slowly toward her.

                    COFFEY
          Ma'am?

                    MELINDA
          Yes, John Coffey?

                    COFFEY
          I see it. I see it.

He comes closer...closer still...

                    MELINDA
                  (a whisper)
          What's happening?

                    COFFEY
          You be still now. You be so quiet
          and so still.

He brushes her forehead with his lips...the gentlest whisper
of a kiss...then moves his mouth down to hers. For a moment we
can see one of her eyes staring past him, filling with an
expression of surprise...

...and then her face is lost to view as Coffey puts his lips
on hers. We hear a soft whistling sound as he begins inhaling
the air deeply from her lungs. Something hot and glowing
starts passing between them, drawn on his breath...

The men watch. The house seems to shudder in that moment, as
if the entire world has shifted an inch to the right...

THE
GREEN
MILE

(CONTINUED)

DOWNSTAIRS PARLOR

...and the grandfather clock stops ticking, the pendulum
stopping dead, the glass face cracking neatly up the center...

BEDROOM

...and a windowpane cracks. Then another. A picture falls off
the wall. A lightbulb bursts, showering glass.

Paul smells smoke, realizes the fringed coverlet of the bed
has caught fire. Moving like a man in a dream, he reaches for
the waterglass on the nightstand, douses the flames.

Coffey keeps kissing Melinda in that deep and mysterious way,
inhaling and inhaling, her hand held in his like a tiny white
bird. For a moment we actually hear something screaming, as if
some willful imp were being extracted by force...

...and then it's over. Coffey raises his head, revealing:

<u>Melinda's</u> <u>beautiful</u> <u>face.</u> Her mouth no longer droops. Color is
coming back to her hair. Her skin is shining with life.

Coffey regards her raptly for a moment or two, then starts
coughing violently. He turns away and drops to his knees,
hacking like a man in the last stages of tuberculosis.

Paul and his men are expecting Coffey to spit out the "bugs,"
but he doesn't -- he just keeps coughing, deep and hard,
barely finding time to snatch in the next breath of air.

Hal goes to his wife, beyond stunned, sits at her side. She
looks back at him with amazement, her face like a dirty mirror
that's been suddenly wiped clean.

John's coughing grows even worse. Brutal drops to his side and
slaps his broad, spasming back.

> BRUTAL
> John! Sick it up! Cough 'em out
> like you done before!

Coffey just keeps retching, eyes watering from the strain,
spit flying from his mouth.

> BRUTAL
> He's choking! Whatever he sucked
> out of her, he's choking on it!

Paul starts toward them. Coffey crawls away, pressing himself
into a corner with his face against the wallpaper. He's still
making gruesome deep hacking sounds, but getting it under
control. He weakly waves Paul off -- let me be.

(CONTINUED)

Paul looks to the bed. Hal sits with Melinda, stroking her brow. Color is blooming in her cheeks even as we watch.

                    MELINDA
          How did I get here? We were going
          to the hospital in Indianola,
          weren't we? We stopped and you
          bought me a packet of wild posies...

                    HAL
          Shhh. It doesn't matter. It
          doesn't matter anymore.

                    MELINDA
          Did I have the X-ray? Did I?

                    PAUL
          Yes.

They both look at him.

                    PAUL
          It was clear. There was no tumor.

Hal bursts into tears. Melinda sits up, comforting him. Her eyes are drawn to the corner.

                    MELINDA
          Who is that man?

Coffey is struggling to rise. Brutal does his best to help.

                    PAUL
          John? Can you turn around? Can you
          turn around and see this lady?

Coffey turns. His face is ashen gray, seriously ill.

                    MELINDA
          What's your name?

                    COFFEY
          John Coffey, ma'am.

                    MELINDA
          Like the drink, only not spelled
          the same.

                    COFFEY
          No, ma'am. Not spelt the same at
          all.

She pushes the covers aside to rise. Hal tries to stop her, but she pushes his hand gently aside. Hal watches in wonder as she stands, takes a first tentative step...and walks to

                              (CONTINUED)

Coffey. She gazes up and touches his face.

> MELINDA
> I dreamed of you. I dreamed you
> were wandering in the dark, and so
> was I. We found each other. We
> found each other in the dark.

She undoes her necklace, holds it up for him. He hesitates,
glances to Paul. Paul nods -- it's all right. Coffey lowers
his head. Melinda affixes the delicate chain around his neck.

> MELINDA
> It's St. Christopher. I want you
> to have it, Mr. Coffey, and wear
> it. He'll keep you safe. Please
> wear it for me.

> COFFEY
> Thank you, ma'am.

> MELINDA
> Thank you, John.

Her arms go around his neck, hugging him tightly as if she
might never let go.

EXT - MOORES HOUSE - NIGHT

Paul and the men hustle Coffey out the front door toward the
truck, helping him as best they can. He's weak as a baby,
knees threatening to give out at any moment.

> PAUL
> C'mon, John, stay on your feet.

> HARRY
> Christ, he goes down, we'll need
> three mules and a crane to pick
> him up again...

They get Coffey to the truck and throw their backs into it,
helping him crawl up onto the stakebed. He rolls over on his
back. Harry hops up, covers him with an old blanket. Brutal
pulls Paul aside, speaking low:

> BRUTAL
> He'll never sit in Old Sparky. You
> know that, don't you?
>   (off Paul's look)
> He swallowed that stuff for a
> reason. I give him a few days. One
> of us'll be doing a cell check and
> there he'll be. Dead on his bunk.

(CONTINUED)

                    PAUL
          If that's his choice, he's earned
          it.
                    (beat)
          Let's get him back on the Mile.

                              FADE TO BLACK

IN BLACKNESS, A TITLE CARD APPEARS:

              "Coffey on the Mile"

                              CUT TO:

INT - E BLOCK - NIGHT

Dean starts babbling with relief as they return:

                    DEAN
          Am I glad to see you! You were
          gone so long! Wild Bill's making
          noises like he's gonna wake up...
                    (notices Coffey)
          What the hell's wrong with him?

                    BRUTAL
          He's hurting, Dean. Hurting bad.

Dean jumps in, helps them steer Coffey into his cell.

                    PAUL
          John, we're gonna set you on your
          bunk now. Ready?

Coffey nods, sits heavily on the bunk. He lowers his head,
breath rasping like a rusted hinge. The guards step out.

                    DEAN
          What about Mrs. Moores? Was it
          like the mouse? Was it a...you
          know...a miracle?

                    PAUL
          Yes. Yes it was.

Paul scans their faces. Smiles are traded. An exultant beat.

                    HARRY
          Damn. I think we got away with it.

                    BRUTAL
          We still gotta convince a certain
          somebody to keep his trap shut.

THE
GREEN
MILE

                              (CONTINUED)

                        PAUL
              Get his stuff.

Dean hurries off to retrieve Percy's holster and baton. Brutal
unlocks the restraint room door, swings it open. Percy is
revealed sitting against the wall, glaring, his mouth still
taped. Paul crouches down. Brutal joins him.

                        PAUL
              I want to talk, not shout. I take
              the tape off, you gonna be calm?

Percy nods. Paul takes hold of the tape, preparing to yank.

                        BRUTAL
              My mother always said if you do it
              fast, it won't hurt so much.

Paul rips the tape off. Percy's eyes water with pain.

                        BRUTAL
              I guess she was wrong.

                        PERCY
              Get me out of this nut-coat.

                        PAUL
              In a minute.

                        PERCY
              Now! Now! Right n--

Paul slaps him hard, knocks him sideways. Percy looks up,
blinking in surprise. Paul grabs him, yanks him back up.

                        PAUL
              You shut up and listen. You
              deserved to be punished for what
              you did to Del. You'll accept it
              like a man, or we'll make you
              sorry you were ever born. We'll
              tell people how you sabotaged
              Del's execution --

                        PERCY
              Sabotaged!

                        PAUL
              -- and how you pissed yourself like
              a frightened little girl. Yes, we'll
              talk, that's a given -- but, Percy,
              mind me now...we'll also see you
              beaten within an inch of your life.

Percy blinks, unable to grasp that.

(CONTINUED)

PAUL
We know people, too, are you so
foolish you don't realize that?
(off Percy's look)
Let bygones be bygones. Nothing's
hurt so far but your pride...and
nobody need ever know about that
except the people in this room.

BRUTAL
What happens on the Mile, stays on
the Mile. Always has.

A long pause. Softly:

PERCY
May I be let out of this coat now?

They pull him to his feet, undo the straps. He shrugs out of
the straitjacket and adjusts his clothes, trying to maintain a
shred of dignity.

PERCY
My things?

Dean hands them over. Percy smoothes his hair and puts his hat
on, starts strapping on his holster belt.

PAUL
Think it over, Percy.

PERCY
Oh, I intend to. I intend to think
about it very hard. Starting right
now.

Percy exits the restraint room. Brutal whispers to Paul:

BRUTAL
He'll talk. Sooner or later.

Paul nods with weary resignation -- yeah, I know.

ON THE MILE

Percy pauses near Coffey's cell, careless as always, getting
his holster buckled -- and a massive black arm grabs him
through the bars. His SCREAM brings Paul and the others
running from the restraint room.

Coffey's face is pressed so tight between his bars it looks
like he's trying to push his head through. He draws his lips
back, baring his teeth in an awful sneer...

THE
GREEN
MILE

Percy whacks him with his baton. Coffey barely seems to feel it. He curls his free hand around the back of Percy's head, pulling him ever closer...

...and Percy's screams are muffled as their mouths come together. Coffey begins exhaling as if he'd held his breath for hours. Percy jerks like a fish on a hook, but can't get away. The men jump in, trying to pry Percy loose, hollering for Coffey to let him go.

The black "insects" are flowing from Coffey to Percy, swirling into his mouth, up his nose, down his throat.

Several lightbulbs explode in their steel cages up and down the Mile. Percy's baton drops from his nerveless fingers and clatters to the floor, never to be picked up again.

And then Coffey steps back, rubbing his mouth as if he's tasted something bad. The color has returned to his skin.

Percy, however, is ashen gray. His expression is blank as a sheet of paper, not a trace of awareness in his eyes.

The men are stunned. Paul raises his hand to Percy's face, snaps his fingers. Nothing. He tries again, clapping loudly. Percy reacts slightly, eyes fluttering, swaying a bit.

> PAUL
> Easy, easy. You all right?

Percy says nothing. He turns and walks slowly up the Mile, his movements vacant and disjointed. He comes to a swaying stop at Wild Bill's cell...and turns slowly to look in.

Wild Bill is coming painfully around, groggily clutching his head. He looks up, sees Percy.

> BILLY
> What'a you looking at, you limp
> noodle? You wanna kiss my ass or
> suck my dick?

Nothing for the longest moment. Percy just staring...

...and then he pulls his gun and empties it into Wild Bill as fast as he can pull the trigger: BAM!BAM!BAM!BAM!BAM!BAM! Bill takes all six rounds in the chest, reeling back across the cell. He hits the wall and slides down, leaving a smear, his face registering a final look of stunned surprise.

Paul and the others tackle Percy and bring him down, wrestling the gun out of his hand. Dean is almost weeping:

> DEAN
> Oh, God, no...

(CONTINUED)

Percy is flat on his back, staring up at nothing. The black "bugs" come drifting out of his nose and mouth, swirling in the air over his head. They turn white and disappear.

The men are speechless. Paul turns, sees Coffey sitting on the floor at his bars, watching.

                    COFFEY
          Punished them bad men. Punished
          'em both.

                    PAUL
          Why Wild Bill? Why?

                    COFFEY
          I saw in his heart. When he grab
          my arm, I saw what Wild Billy
          done. Saw plain as day. Can't hide
          what's in your heart.

                    PAUL
          What? Saw what?

Coffey reaches toward him, straining through the bars.

                    COFFEY
          Take my hand, boss. You see for
          yourself.

                    BRUTAL
          Paul, no!

Paul hesitates, torn between reason and Coffey's pleading eyes. A whisper:

                    COFFEY
          My hand.

Paul can't help it. He has to. Their hands come together. Paul lurches wildly as that circuit starts blazing between them...

                    PAUL
          No...please...

                    COFFEY
          Gots to, boss. Gots to give you a
          little bit of myself. A gift,
          like. A gift of what's inside me
          so you can see too...

...and Paul sees:

The Detterick twins. Kathe and Cora. Laughing and playing hopscotch in the dust under a late afternoon sun...

A dinner table. Family having supper late in the day, basket of biscuits being passed. 12 year-old Howie Detterick taking it, passing it on...

A hand with a paint brush slopping bright red paint on the side of a barn...

Kathe skipping to the head of the hopscotch squares, turning and starting back, laughing in the sun...

The paint brush slopping more paint, dripping like blood...

Paul jerks and twists, trying to pull away, trying to break the circuit, but he can't, not till all is seen and done:

Marjorie Detterick calling from the porch for everybody to come eat, supper's ready...

A hammer pausing. Klaus looking down from atop the barn...

The Detterick twins finishing their hopscotch, gathering their jump-ropes from the dust, running across the yard...

The basket of biscuits being passed to little Cora, who takes a biscuit and passes it on...

Klaus coming down the ladder, calling to his daughters. The little girls running past the man with the paintbrush, who turns and smiles as they go by...it's Wild Bill.

The basket of biscuits is passed one last time. A hand pulls one out, raises it for a bite. It's Wild Bill, smiling at the little girls as conversation flows around the table...

Paul screams, trying to pull away, but:

The porch door is kicked off its hinges just before dawn, a figure looming in the doorway. Kathe wakes, her scream cut short as a man's fist punches her hard in the face...

Paul trembles violently as if riding the lightning himself, pleading for it stop, but there's one last thing:

Wild Bill looms over the terrified little girls like a horrendous boogeyman, whispers to Kathe:

> BILLY
> You love your sister? You make any
> noise, you know what happens? I'll
> kill her instead of you.
> (to Cora)
> And if you make any noise, I'll
> kill her.

And he drags them out into the coming dawn...

(CONTINUED)

...<u>as</u> <u>Coffey</u> <u>lets</u> <u>Paul</u> <u>go.</u> Paul is gasping, back in the real
world where his men are staring at him with wide eyes.

> COFFEY
> He kill 'em with they love. They love
> for each other. You see how it is?

Paul nods, numb. Tears are flowing down Coffey's face. Softly:

> COFFEY
> That's how it is ever' day. That's
> how it is all over the worl'...

> CUT TO:

WILD BILL

lies dead, staring with glassy eyes. A FLASHBULB POPS, rimming
him with harsh blue light...

INT - E BLOCK - DAWN

...as Hal arrives, wearing his pajama top under his overcoat.
He sees the POLICE PHOTOGRAPHER taking pictures. The guards
are giving statements to GROUPS OF COPS, everybody murmuring:

> DEAN
> ...well, I dunno, he just snapped,
> I guess...

> HARRY
> ...s'right, one minute he's fine,
> the next -- blammo...

> BRUTAL
> ...bastard grabbed him through the
> bars a few days back, scared the
> boy so bad he wet himself...

Hal turns, sees:

PERCY

sits handcuffed on the floor of the Mile, eyes glassier than
Wild Bill's. TWO COPS are trying to snap him out of it:

> COP #1
> Son! <u>Son!</u> Can you hear me?

> COP #2
> Speak up if you can hear us! We
> gotta ask you some questions!

A MEDIC is raising Percy's eyelid with his thumb, shining a
penlight, getting no reaction.

(CONTINUED)

                         MEDIC
          I think this boy's cheese slid off
          his cracker.

HAL

sees Paul, motions him aside to talk privately:

                         HAL
          I'll cover you as much as I can,
          even if it means my job, but I
          have to know. Does this have
          anything do with what happened at
          my house? Does it, Paul?

Paul looks Hal in the eye. As with Bitterbuck, the lie comes
easy:

                         PAUL
          No.

                                        CUT TO:

INT - HOSPITAL ROOM - DAY

TRACKING A PAIR OF FEET shuffling into the room in hospital
slippers, escorted by TWO ORDERLIES. The patient is brought to
a window. The orderlies turn and leave...

...and we BOOM UP to reveal Percy, catatonic, staring out the
same window where we met Wild Bill...

EXT - HOSPITAL - DAY

...and we WIDEN SLOWLY from Percy at the window to reveal his
last stop in life. It's emblazoned on the gate: BRIAR RIDGE
MENTAL HOSPITAL. He finally got that transfer.

                                        DISSOLVE TO:

INT - KITCHEN - NIGHT

Paul is at the kitchen table in the wee hours, listening to
the radio as usual, sipping beer. Jan comes down, miserable
and exhausted, wishing there was comfort she could offer. She
joins him at the table.

                         JAN
          Does Hal know? That Coffey's
          innocent, I mean?
                 (Paul shakes his head)
          Can he help? Does he have the
          influence to do something about
          this? Stop the execution?

                                        (CONTINUED)

                    PAUL
No.

                    JAN
Then don't tell him. If he can't
help, don't tell him. Ever.

                    PAUL
I won't.

                    JAN
          (beat)
There's no way out of this for
you, is there?

                    PAUL
No. I've been thinking about it,
too, believe me. Run it through my
head any number of ways.
          (beat)
Tell you the truth, honey. I've
done some things in my life I'm
not proud of, but this is the
first time I've ever felt in real
danger of hell.

                    JAN
Hell? Oh, Paul...
          (touches his face)
Talk to him. Talk to John. Find
out what he wants.

                                        CUT TO:

INT - E BLOCK - NIGHT

Coffey sits quietly in his cell, a solitary firefly flitting
in circles around his finger. Paul and the men appear. The
firefly flits away, vanishing through Coffey's tiny window.

                    COFFEY
Hello, boss.

                    PAUL
Hello, John.

Brutal unlocks the cell. Paul enters.

                    PAUL
I guess you know we're coming down
to it now. Another couple of days.
          (beat)
Is there anything special you'd
like for dinner that night? We can
rustle you up most anything.

                              (CONTINUED)

Coffey gives it some careful thought.

>   COFFEY
>   Meatloaf be nice. Mashed taters
>   with gravy. Okra. Maybe some'a
>   that fine cornbread your missus
>   make, if she don' mind.

>   PAUL
>   What about a preacher? Someone you
>   could say a little prayer with?

>   COFFEY
>   Don't want no preacher. You can
>   say a prayer, if ya want. I could
>   get kneebound wit you, I guess.

>   PAUL
>   Me?

Coffey gives him a look -- please.

>   PAUL
>   S'pose I could, if it came to that.

Paul sits, working himself up to it:

>   PAUL
>   John, I have to ask you something
>   very important now.

>   COFFEY
>   I know what you gonna say. You
>   don' have to say it.

>   PAUL
>   I do. I do have to.
>   (beat)
>   John, tell me what you want me to
>   do. You want me to take you out of
>   here? Just let you run away? See
>   how far you can get?

>   COFFEY
>   Why would you do such a foolish
>   thing?

Paul hesitates, emotions swirling, trying to find the words.

>   PAUL
>   On the day of my judgment, when I
>   stand before God, and He asks me
>   why did I kill one of his true
>   miracles, what am I gonna say?
>   That it was my job? My job?

(CONTINUED)

                              COFFEY
                You tell God the Father it was a
                kindness you done.
                         (takes his hand)
                I know you hurtin' and worryin'. I
                can feel it on you, but you
                oughtta quit on it now. Because I
                <u>want</u> it over and done. I do.

Coffey hesitates -- now <u>he's</u> the one trying to find the right
words, trying to make Paul understand:

                              COFFEY
                I's tired, boss. Tired of bein' on
                the road, lonely as a sparrow in
                the rain. Tired of not ever having
                me a buddy to be with, or tell me
                where we's coming from or going
                to, or why. Mostly I'm tired of
                people being ugly to each other.
                I'm tired of all the pain I feel
                and hear in the world ever' day.
                There's too much of it. It's like
                pieces of glass in my head all the
                time. Can you understand?

By now, Paul is blinking back tears. Softly:

                              PAUL
                Yes, John. I think I can.

                              BRUTAL
                There must be something we can do
                for you, John. There must be
                something you want.

Coffey thinks about this long and hard, finally looks up.

                              COFFEY
                I ain't never seen me a flicker
                show.

                                        CUT TO:

TIGHT ON COFFEY'S FACE

gazing with wide-eyed, open-mouthed wonder, the light of a
motion picture projector flickering on his skin...

INT - PRISON AUDITORIUM - NIGHT

...while Fred Astaire and Ginger Rogers dance up there on the
big screen, images flowing in magical black and silver tones.

THE
GREEN
MILE

                              (CONTINUED)

                         ASTAIRE
                        (singing)
           Heaven, I'm in heaven...and my
           heart beats so that I can hardly
           speak...

Paul and the men are scattered about in the otherwise empty
auditorium, also watching.

PROJECTION BOOTH

Toot operates the projector, peering through the tiny window
into the theater. He yawns, glances at his watch. Late.

IN THE AUDITORIUM

Fred and Ginger are now in the most passionate and graceful
part of the dance. Irving Berlin's music swells.

COFFEY

can't believe what he's seeing. He's so excited his breath is
caught in his throat. Softly:

                         COFFEY
           Why, they's angels. Angels. Just
           like up in heaven...

                                        DISSOLVE TO:

INT - E BLOCK - NIGHT

FOUR PAIRS OF FEET come marching up the Green Mile.

ANGLE ON COFFEY

Paul appears at the bars with Brutal, Harry, and Dean. Nothing
is said. Coffey knows why they're here. He rises as Brutal
unlocks the cell, slides the door open. Coffey steps out,
looks around at their dazed and sad faces.

                         COFFEY
           I be all right, fellas. This
           here's the hard part. I be all
           right in a little while.

Paul indicates the St. Christopher medal around John's neck:

                         PAUL
           John, I should have that just for
           now. I'll give it back after.

John lets him take the necklace. Paul pockets it. They start
to walk the Mile as:

THE
GREEN
MILE

                                        (CONTINUED)

                    COFFEY
        You know, I fell asleep this
        afternoon and had me a dream. I
        dreamed about Del's mouse.

                    PAUL
        Did you, John?

                    COFFEY
        I dreamed he got down to that
        place Boss Howell talk about, that
        Mouseville place. I dreamed there
        was kids, and how they laughed at
        his tricks! My!

He laughs at the memory of it, then grows more serious:

                    COFFEY
        I dreamed those two little blonde-
        headed girls were there. They 'us
        laughing, too. I put my arms
        around 'em and sat 'em on my
        knees, and there 'us no blood
        comin' outta their hair and they
        'us fine. We all watch Mr. Jingles
        roll that spool, and how we did
        laugh. Fit to bus', we was.

Behind them, Dean stifles a sob.

PAUL'S INNER OFFICE

Coffey kneels. Paul joins him, self-conscious and uncertain.

                    PAUL
        What should we pray for, John?

                    COFFEY
        Strength?

Paul nods -- strength it is. Harry surprises Brutal and Dean
by also kneeling. Brutal and Dean hesitate...then join them.

                    PAUL
        God, please help us finish what
        we've started, and please welcome
        this man, John Coffey -- like the
        drink, but not spelled the same --
        into heaven and give him peace.
        Please help us to see him off the
        best we can and let nothing go
        wrong. Amen.

Paul starts to rise, but Coffey takes his hand.

THE
GREEN
MILE

                    (CONTINUED)

>   COFFEY
> I know a prayer I once heard. Can
> I say it?

>   PAUL
> You go right ahead, John. Take all
> the time you need.

Coffey closes his eyes, frowning in deep concentration.

>   COFFEY
> Baby Jesus, meek and mild, pray
> for me...

And <u>Paul</u> sees:

Kathe and Cora Detterick kneeling together in the enclosed
porch that night, just before their bedtime:

>   KATHE AND CORA
> ...and every child. Be my
> strength, be my friend...

And then the vision is gone as:

>   COFFEY
> ...be with me until the end. Amen.

Coffey rises, offers Paul his hand, helps him up.

EXECUTION CHAMBER

Full house tonight. Bill Dodge is waiting at Old Sparky.

Silence as Coffey is led in, all eyes on him. Klaus and
Marjorie Detterick are in the front row. She mutters:

>   MARJORIE
> Die slow, you bastard.

COFFEY

is faltering as Paul and Brutal bring him to the chair.

>   COFFEY
> They's a lot of folks here hate
> me. A <u>lot.</u> I can feel it. Like
> bees stinging me. It <u>hurts.</u>

>   BRUTAL
> Feel how <u>we</u> feel, then. We don't
> hate you -- can you feel that?

Coffey tries to take comfort in it, but flinches as:

(CONTINUED)

                              KLAUS
              Kill him twice, you boys! You go
              on and kill that raping baby-
              killer twice, that'd be fine!

Marjorie dissolves into tears. Klaus pulls her against his
shoulder, looking dazed by the whole thing.

Paul and Brutal turn John around, sit him down. Paul notices
Dean crying again, his back to the witnesses. They kneel to
apply the leg clamps, while Brutal and Harry secure the arms.

                              PAUL
              Wipe your face before you stand
              up, Dean.

Dean nods, wiping his face with the sleeve of his coat. They
rise, stepping back. This time, Paul's out front:

                              PAUL
              Roll on one.

Van Hay cranks the generator. The lights flare hotter and
brighter. It's just like in Melinda's bedroom the night Coffey
cured her with a kiss. Airless and bright, dreamlike.

                              MARJORIE
              Does it hurt, yet? I hope it does!
              I hope it hurts like hell!

                              PAUL
              John Coffey...you have been
              condemned to die in the electric
              chair by a jury of your peers...
              sentence imposed by a judge
              in good standing in this state. Do
              you have anything to say before
              sentence is carried out?

                              COFFEY
              I'm sorry for what I am.

                              MARJORIE
              You ought to be! Oh, you monster,
              you damn well ought to be!

Brutal takes the mask from the hook to draw it over Coffey's
head. Coffey looks to Paul with terrified, pleading eyes.

                              COFFEY
              Please, boss, don't put that thing
              over my face. Don't put me in the
              dark, I's afraid of the dark.

THE
GREEN
MILE

121

(CONTINUED)

> PAUL
> All right, John.

Brutal puts the mask back, proceeds with the sponge.

IN TIGHT ANGLES:

The cap is lowered, the straps drawn. Coffey is breathing fast, terrified, muttering under his breath:

> COFFEY
> ...heaven...I'm in heaven...
> heaven...heaven...heaven...

THE WITNESSES

sit and wait, barely breathing.

JACK VAN HAY

is poised at the switch, wondering why the order won't come.

PAUL

is staring at Coffey, unable to say the words.

> BRUTAL
> (whispers)
> Paul. You have to say it. You have
> to give the order.

Paul can't. He reaches out and touches Coffey's hand. Their fingers clasp. In that moment, staring into his eyes, Paul hears the last thought that ever goes through Coffey's head:

> COFFEY'S VOICE
> (whispered V.O.)
> *He kill 'em with they love. That's*
> *how it is ever' day. All over the*
> *worl'...*

Their fingers disengage. Paul steps back, eyes still locked with Coffey's, and says the hardest words he's ever spoken:

> PAUL
> Roll on two.

Van Hay throws the switch. Coffey surges forward, fingers splayed and jittering past Old Sparky's arms.

Lights begin blowing out all over the Mile, raining shattered glass and sparks. Some of the witnesses scream.

A thin line of blood comes trickling out of Klaus Detterick's nose. He reaches up, absently wipes it away.

THE
GREEN
MILE

122

(CONTINUED)

Coffey's eyes are locked on Paul's, riding the lightning all the way. He finally slumps. Van Hay kills the current.

Coffey's expression is peaceful, as if sleeping. A final pair of tears drift gently down his cheeks.

INT - ACCESS TUNNEL - NIGHT

Paul carefully replaces the St. Christopher's medal around Coffey's neck. Brutal wheels the body down the tunnel as

> OLD PAUL (V.O.)
> That was the last execution I ever took part in...

> CUT TO:

INT - NURSING HOME SUNROOM - PRESENT DAY

The rain has stopped. It's late in the day.

> PAUL
> ...just couldn't do it anymore after that. Brutal either. We both transferred out, took jobs with Boys' Correctional.
> (beat, nods)
> That was all right. Catch 'em young, that became my motto. Might even have done some good.

ANGLE SHIFTS TO Elaine listening. Uncertain.

> PAUL
> You don't believe me.

> ELAINE
> I don't imagine you would lie to me, Paul. It's just that...

> PAUL
> ...it's quite a story.

> ELAINE
> Yes. Quite a story.
> (pause)
> One thing I don't understand. You said you and Jan had a grown son in 1935. Is that right?

> PAUL
> (nods)
> He was nineteen that year.

THE GREEN MILE

(CONTINUED)

                    ELAINE
        But if that's true...

                    PAUL
        The math doesn't work, does it?

She shakes her head. Paul thinks, comes to a decision.

                    PAUL
        Feel up to a walk?

                              CUT TO:

EXT - WOODS - DAY

Paul and Elaine, both wearing ponchos, come along the wooded
path into view of the storage shacks.

INT - SHACK - DAY

We see Paul approach through the grimy window as before, this
time bringing Elaine. ANGLE SHIFTS to the door as they arrive,
creaking open on rusty hinges to reveal them.

They enter. She looks around at the musty nooks and crannies,
wondering what they're doing here. Paul touches her arm.

                    PAUL
        There.

Elaine moves closer, sees it on the dusty floorboards:

An old cigar box.

For a moment, she doesn't know what to make of it.

                    PAUL
        Hey. Wake up, old boy. Wake up.

Elaine's breath catches in her throat...

...as a pair of bright oilspot eyes peer over the edge of the
cigar box. It's a mouse. His fur, once brown, is now all gray.

                    ELAINE
        Paul? It isn't...it can't be...

Paul gets down on the floor, holds out his hand.

                    PAUL
        Come over here, boy. Come on over
        here and see this lady.

The mouse tries several times to get over the side of the
cigar box before he finally makes it. He comes to them,

                              (CONTINUED)

hobbling and crippled with arthritis.

                         ELAINE
               That can't be Mr. Jingles.

Paul says nothing, just pulls a spool from his pocket. Mr.
Jingles might be old, but he's as obsessed as ever. He gets
ready to fetch, eyes riveted to the spool. Softly:

                         PAUL
               Messieurs et mesdames. Bienvenue
               au cirque du mousie.

Paul tosses the spool. The mouse limps painfully after it. He
reaches it, goes around...and has to lay down to catch his
breath. Elaine starts forward, but Paul holds her back.

After a moment, Mr. Jingles finds his feet again. He rises and
starts nosing the spool back to Paul.

                         ELAINE
               Oh, Paul. Don't make him do it
               again.

                         PAUL
                    (softly)
               But he loves it so much.

He glances around at the shack with a sad smile.

                         PAUL
               This isn't exactly the Mouseville
               we had in mind...but we make do,
               don't we, old fella?

He breaks off a crumb of toast for the mouse. Mr. Jingles
stretches forward, carefully starts to eat.

                         PAUL
               I think Mr. Jingles happened by
               accident. I think when we
               electrocuted Del, and it all went
               so badly...well, John could <u>feel</u>
               it happening, you know...and I
               think a small part of whatever
               magic was inside of him just leapt
               into my tiny friend here...
                    (beat)
               As for me...well, John had to give
               me a part of himself...a gift, the
               way he saw it...so I could see for
               myself what Wild Bill had done.
               When John did that...when he took
               my hand...a part of the power that
               worked through him spilled into me.

THE
GREEN
MILE

                    (CONTINUED)

                    ELAINE
          He...what? _Infected_ you with life?

Paul looks at the mouse, strokes him gently between the ears.

                    PAUL
          That's as good a word as any. He
          infected us both, didn't he, Mr.
          Jingles? With life.
                    (beat)
          I'm a hundred and eight years old,
          Elaine. I was forty four the year
          John Coffey walked the Green Mile.

                    ELAINE
          ...oh my God...

CAMERA PUSHES SLOWLY IN on Paul as:

                    PAUL
          You musn't blame John. He couldn't
          have known what would happen. He
          was just a...force of nature.
                    (beat)
          I've lived to see amazing things,
          Ellie. Miraculous things. A new
          century come to pass. But I've had
          to watch my friends and loved ones
          die off through the years...Hal
          and Melinda...Brutus Howell...my
          wife...my son...
                    (beat)
          ...and you, Elaine. You'll die,
          too, and my curse is knowing I'll
          be there to see it...

INT - FUNERAL HOME - DAY

Elaine Connelly lies in an open casket.

                    PAUL (V.O.)
          That's my atonement, you see? My
          punishment for letting John Coffey
          ride the lightning...for killing a
          miracle of God...

ANGLE SHIFTS to reveal Paul as he lays a rose atop the casket.

                    PAUL (V.O.)
          ...you'll be gone, like all the
          others, and I'll have to stay...

                                             (CONTINUED)

EXT - CEMETERY - DAY

Paul stands at the graveside as the casket is lowered.

                    PAUL (V.O.)
          I'll die eventually, of that I'm
          sure. I have no illusions of
          immortality. But I will have
          wished for death long before death
          finds me.

He turns and walks away.

                    PAUL (V.O.)
          In truth, I wish for it already.

INT - E BLOCK - NIGHT (1935)

Empty and silent. Young Paul walks the Mile alone, listening
to the quiet. He pauses, seeing something. A whisper:

                    PAUL
          Mr. Jingles?

It is Mr. Jingles. The little mouse is peering from under the
restraint room door. He's come home, looking bedraggled. Paul
bends down, gently picks him up.

                    PAUL
          Where you been, boy? I've been
          worried about you. You hungry?
          Let's find you something to eat...

Paul turns and heads back up the Green Mile, carrying the
mouse cupped in his hands as we

                              MATCH DISSOLVE TO:

INT - NURSING HOME - PRESENT DAY

Young Paul transforms into Old Paul in the dissolve, the
corridor of the Green Mile becoming the corridor of the
nursing home. He's returning from the funeral.

                    PAUL (V.O.)
          I lie in bed most nights, thinking
          about it. And I wait...

INT - PAUL'S BEDROOM - NIGHT

Paul lies unable to sleep. He rolls over, staring at the moon
outside his window.

                                        (CONTINUED)

                    PAUL (V.O.)
          I think about all the people I've
          loved, now long gone. I think
          about my beautiful Jan, and how I
          lost her so many years ago. I think
          about all of us walking our own
          Green Mile, each in our own time.
          But one thought, more than any
          other, keeps me awake most nights...
                    (beat)
          ...if he could make a mouse live
          so long, how much longer do I have?

INT - SHACK - NIGHT

SLOW TRACKING SHOT takes us across the dusty floorboards
toward an ancient cigar box lying in a spill of moonlight and
shadow...

                    PAUL (V.O.)
          We each owe a death, there are no
          exceptions...but sometimes, oh God,
          the Green Mile seems so long...

...and CAMERA peeks in to reveal Mr. Jingles sleeping fitfully
in the box, chasing that spool in his dreams as we

                                        FADE OUT

                    THE END

STILLS

Clockwise from top: 1) Tom Hanks stars as Paul Edgecomb, supervisor of death row at Cold Mountain Penitentiary. 2) Michael Clarke Duncan portrays John Coffey, the childlike inmate with mysterious healing powers. 3) Bonnie Hunt as Janice Edgecomb, Paul's wife. 4) David Morse as Brutus "Brutal" Howell, Paul's friend and fellow guard.

Clockwise from top: 1) James Cromwell and Patricia Clarkson portray Warden Hal Moores and wife Melinda. 2) Michael Jeter plays Eduard Delacroix, the Cajun inmate who adopts a pet mouse. 3) Jeffrey DeMunn as guard Harry Terwilliger. 4) Doug Hutchison as sadistic guard Percy Wetmore, nephew of the governor.

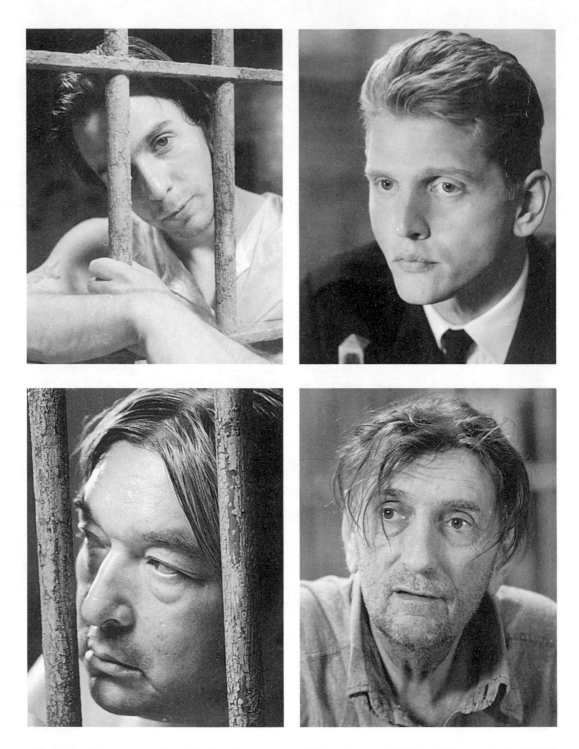

Clockwise from top: 1) Sam Rockwell portrays problem inmate William Wharton, aka "Wild Bill." 2) Barry Pepper as Dean Stanton, the youngest guard on the Mile. 3) Veteran character actor Harry Dean Stanton plays Toot-Toot, the crazy old trusty. 4) Graham Greene as inmate Arlen Bitterbuck.

Top: Marking his one hundredth big-screen appearance, veteran actor Dabbs Greer portrays old Paul Edgecomb in the wrap-around segments. Fellow veteran Eve Brent plays his friend, Elaine Connelly.

Bottom: John Coffey is led into the execution chamber.

Top: Dedicated extras toil in the Tennessee heat to portray chain-ganged convicts in 1935.
Bottom: Mule wrangler Malcolm Jessup and his team lend an air of authenticity to the work field.

Top: A *Green Mile* family portrait, left to right: Barry Pepper, David Morse, Bonnie Hunt, Tom Hanks, Jeffrey DeMunn, director Frank Darabont.

Bottom: Cinematographer David Tattersall, seen here on location in Tennessee, is responsible for the extraordinary photography of *The Green Mile*.

Top: Camera operator David Emmerichs (left, with Steadicam) and the director line up a shot during night-filming in Tennessee. Note the platformed walkway built to make actor Michael Clarke Duncan (John Coffey) appear even larger than he is in real life.

Bottom: Darabont confers with Michael Clarke Duncan.

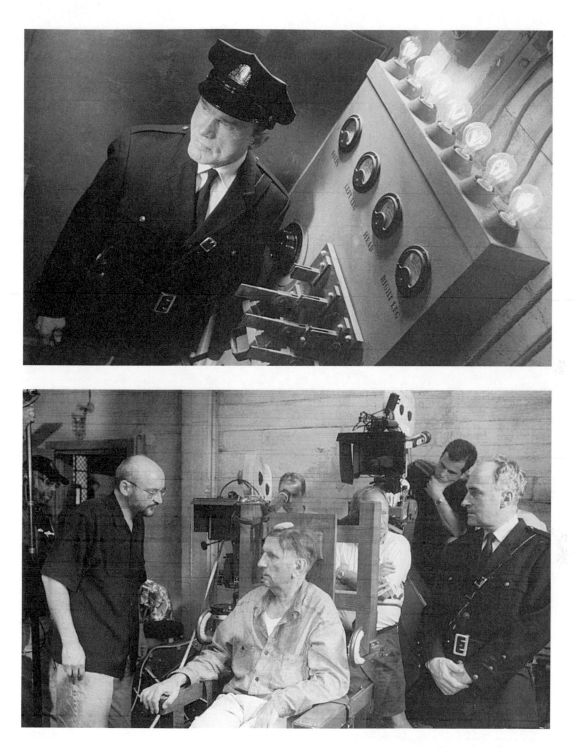

Top: Executioner Jack Van Hay (actor Bill McKinney) awaits the signal to throw the switch.
Bottom: Planning a shot for the "execution rehearsal" scene. Actor Harry Dean Stanton sits in
Old Sparky, patiently awaiting direction with a sponge atop his head.

Top: Darabont, Hanks, and Stanton between takes.
Bottom: Stephen King gets a surprise birthday cake from the cast and crew while visiting the *Green Mile* set in Los Angeles.

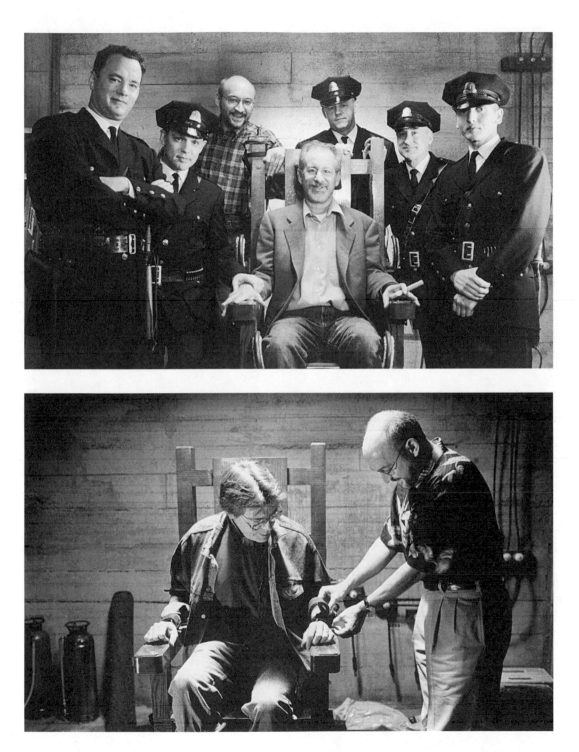

Top: Never let it be said we don't know how to treat distinguished visitors to the Mile—here, Steven Spielberg gets the hot seat from his fans. From left to right are Tom Hanks, Doug Hutchison, Frank Darabont, Steven Spielberg, David Morse, Jeff DeMunn, and Barry Pepper.
Bottom: Another example of VIP treatment as Stephen King gets strapped into Old Sparky.

THE
GREEN
MILE

139

Top: The Edgecombs pay a visit to Hal and Melinda Moores.
Bottom: Eduard Delacroix (Michael Jeter) says farewell to his beloved pet mouse before walking
the last mile.

Top: Discussing a shot at the monitors, from left to right, are visual effects supervisor Charles Gibson, producer David Valdes, Darabont, script supervisor Susan Malerstein-Watkins, Tom Hanks, and David Morse.

Bottom: Watching the mouse arrive on the Mile.

Top: Darabont confers with Bonnie Hunt during location filming in Tennessee.
Bottom: Working out the blocking of a scene with James Cromwell on the tunnel set.

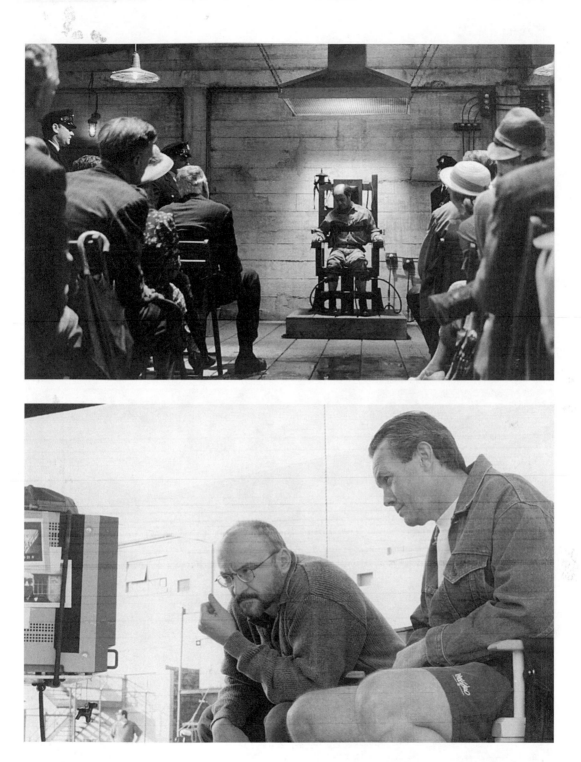

Top: Production designer Terence Marsh's amazing set work is seen to good advantage here. It should be noted that—with the minor exception of the warden's office—every interior of *The Green Mile* was designed and built from scratch by two-time Academy Award–winner Marsh.
Bottom: Producer David Valdes (right) joins Darabont at the monitors.

Top: The KNB Effects crew, hidden behind the execution chamber wall, prepares to operate the articulated dummy used for the fiery climax of Eduard Delacroix's execution. The "Del" dummy was created by KNB's Greg Nicotero and Howard Berger, while the startling flame effects were courtesy of *Green Mile* special effects coordinator Darrell Pritchett.

Bottom: The execution chamber set fills with cast and crew waiting to see the Delacroix dummy's flaming demise.

STORYBOARDS

On the following pages are two of *The Green Mile*'s storyboarded sequences, drawn by artist Peter Von Sholly in consultation with director Frank Darabont. One of the sequences (scene 44: "Percy Tries to Catch the Mouse") does not exist in the finished film—deemed expendable by Darabont, it was dropped from the production schedule and never shot. The other sequence (scene 81: "Paul Gets Healed") appears in the film as rendered.

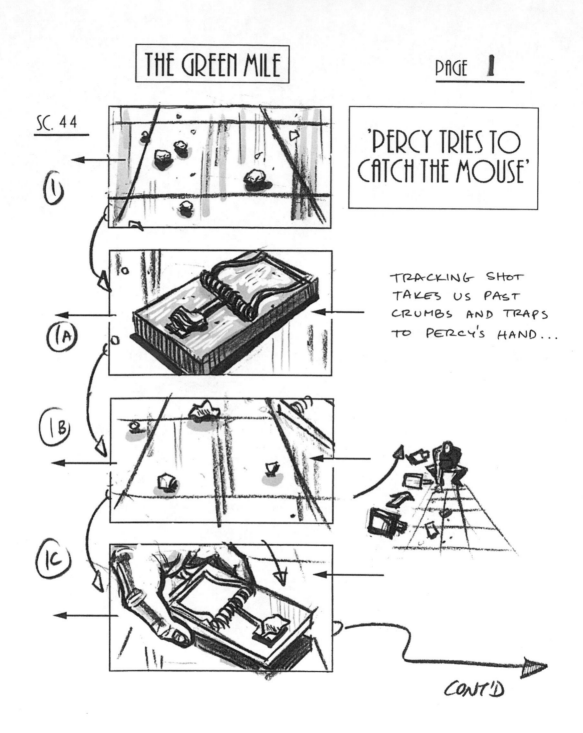

THE GREEN MILE

SC. 44

'PERCY TRIES TO CATCH THE MOUSE'

TRACKING SHOT
TAKES US PAST
CRUMBS AND TRAPS
TO PERCY'S HAND...

CONT'D

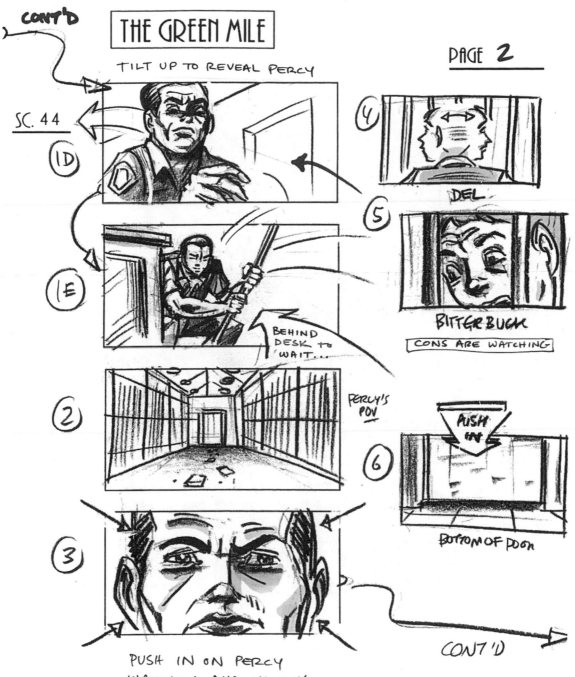

THE GREEN MILE

CON'D

TILT UP TO REVEAL PERCY

PAGE **2**

SC. 44

(1D)

(1E)

BEHIND DESK to WAIT...

(2)

PERCY'S POV

(3)

PUSH IN ON PERCY
WATCHING AND WAITING...

(4)

DEL

(5)

BITTER BUCK

CONS ARE WATCHING

(6)

PUSH IN

BOTTOM OF DOOR

CON'D

THE GREEN MILE

CAMERA BOOMS DOWN FROM PERCY TO REVEAL MOUSE UNDER DESK

CONT.

PAGE 3

SC. 44

3A

MOUSE CREEPS OUT FROM UNDER DESK...

1

... PERCY DOESN'T NOTICE.

(HOLD THESE SHOTS UNTIL MOUSE RUNS)

2

2A

REVERSE ANGLE OF SAME — MOUSE EASES INTO FOREGROUND, LARGE IN FRAME.

(SPECIAL LENS REQUIRED?)

HOLD THRU RUN!

2B

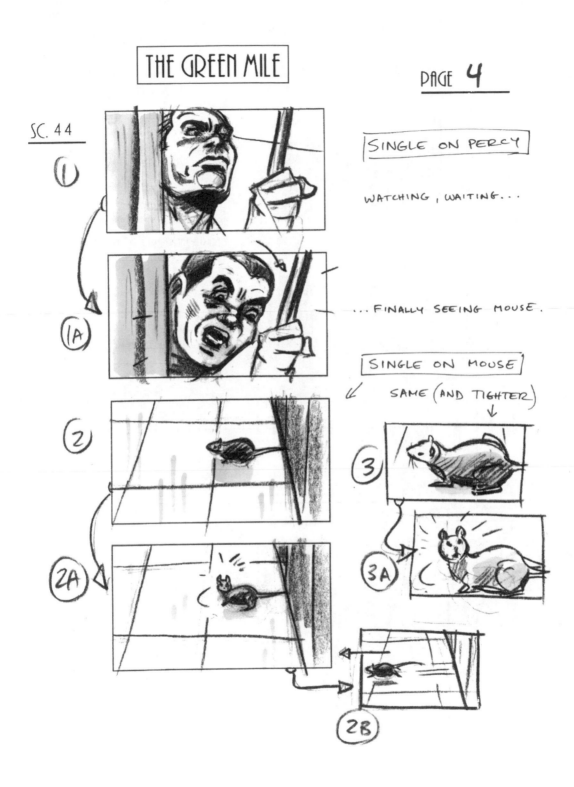

THE GREEN MILE

SC. 44

①

ⒶⒶ 1A

② 2

Ⓐ 2A

Ⓑ 2B

SINGLE ON PERCY

WATCHING, WAITING...

...FINALLY SEEING MOUSE.

SINGLE ON MOUSE

SAME (AND TIGHTER)

③ 3

Ⓐ 3A

THE GREEN MILE

SC. 44

PERCY CHASES
MOUSE TOWARD CAM,
SWATTING WITH BROOM.

PERCY WIPES PAST
BITTERBUCK'S CELL...

THE GREEN MILE

SC. 44

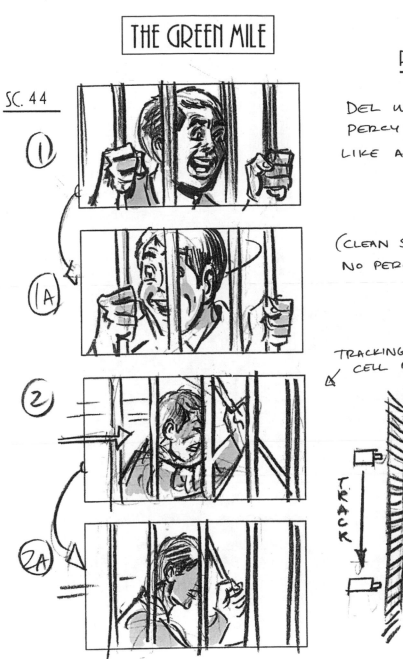

DEL WATCHES
PERCY RUN BY
LIKE A LUNATIC...

(CLEAN SHOT OF DEL,
NO PERCY IN FRAME)

TRACKING PERCY THRU
CELL BARS (FAST!)

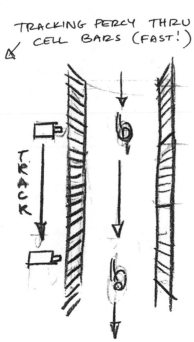

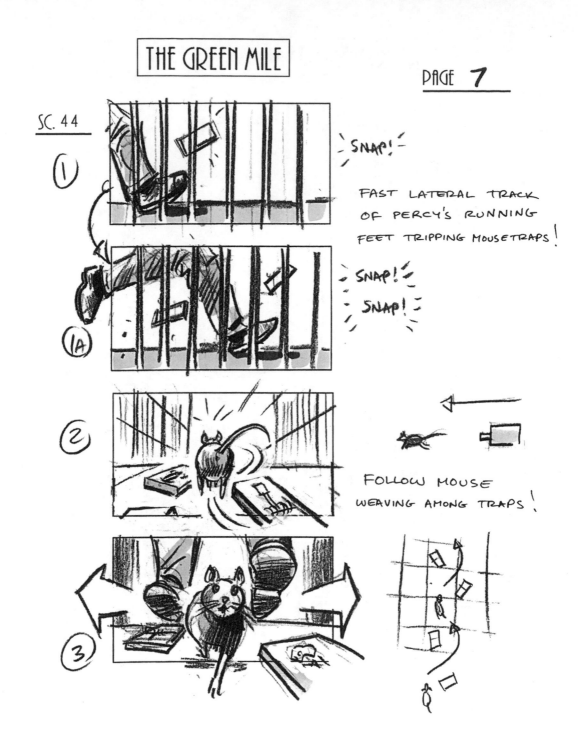

THE GREEN MILE

SC. 44

① SNAP!

FAST LATERAL TRACK
OF PERCY'S RUNNING
FEET TRIPPING MOUSETRAPS!

①A SNAP!
SNAP!

② FOLLOW MOUSE
WEAVING AMONG TRAPS!

③

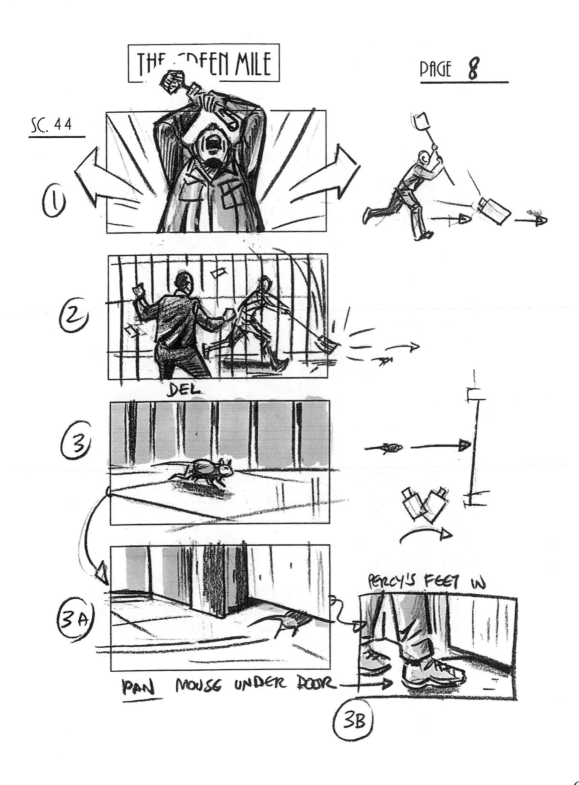

SC. 44

① ② ③

DEL

③A

PAN MOUSE UNDER DOOR

PERCY'S FEET IN

③B

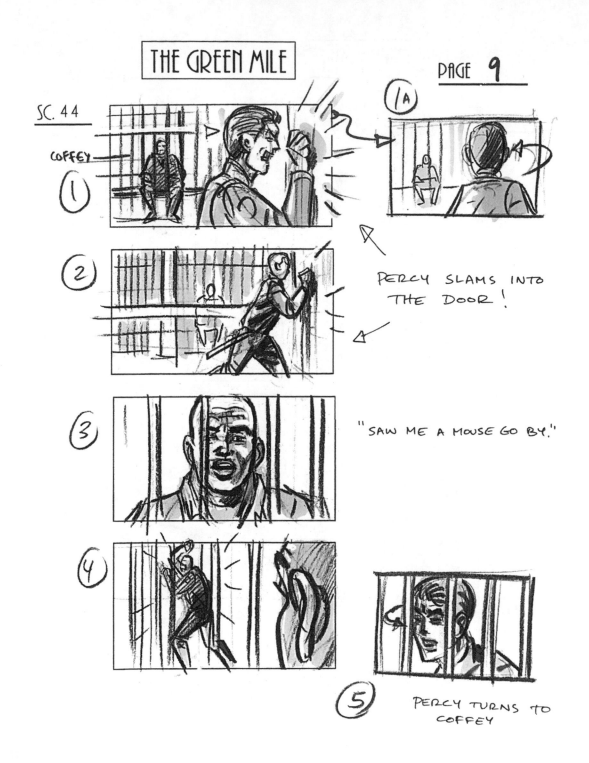

THE GREEN MILE

SC. 44

COFFEY

① 1A

② PERCY SLAMS INTO THE DOOR!

③ "SAW ME A MOUSE GO BY."

④

⑤ PERCY TURNS TO COFFEY

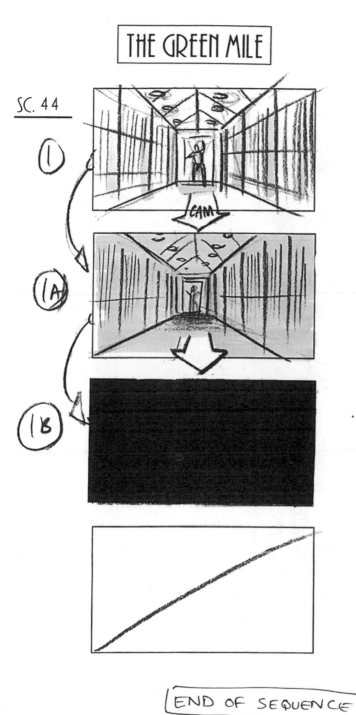

THE GREEN MILE

SC. 44

① ② ③

CAMERA PULLS SLOWLY
BACK AS PERCY GOES
NUTS POUNDING ON
THE DOOR...

...AND WE FADE TO
BLACK ON HIS YELLS,

END OF SEQUENCE

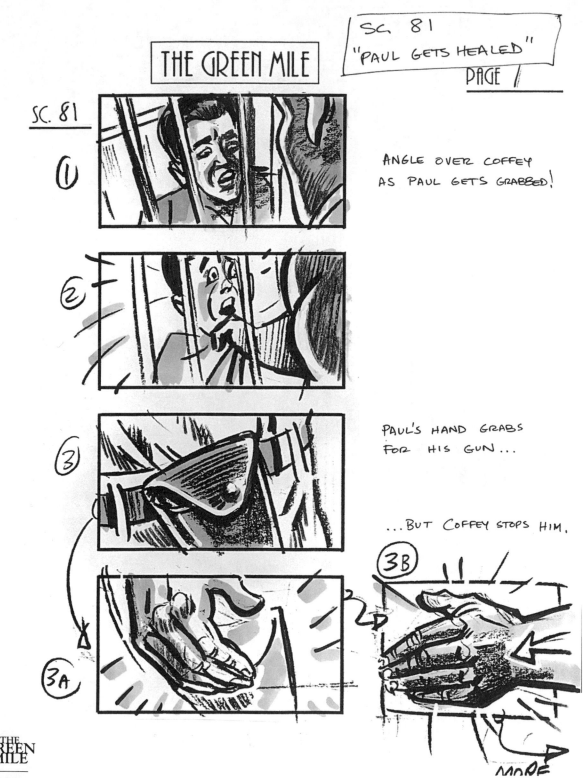

THE GREEN MILE

SC. 81

① ANGLE OVER COFFEY
AS PAUL GETS GRABBED!

②

③ PAUL'S HAND GRABS
FOR HIS GUN...

...BUT COFFEY STOPS HIM.

3B

3A

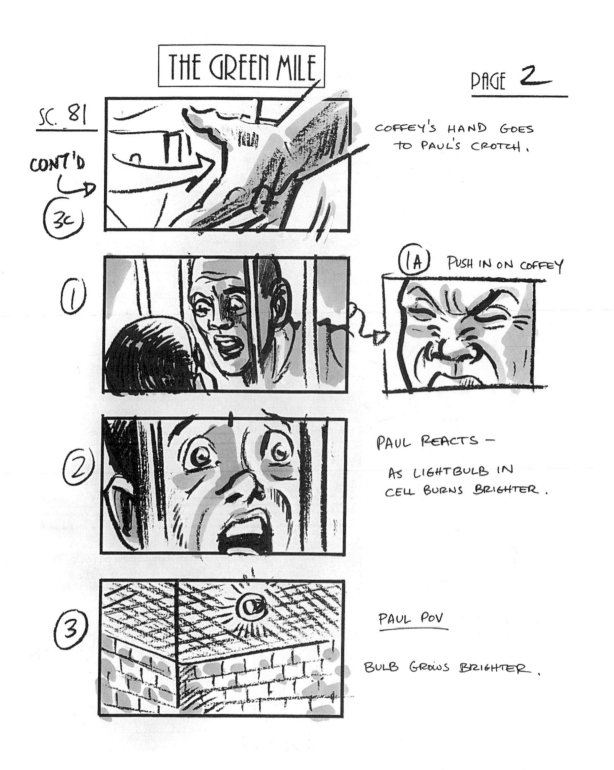

THE GREEN MILE

SC. 81

CONT'D

3C

COFFEY'S HAND GOES TO PAUL'S CROTCH.

1

1A PUSH IN ON COFFEY

2

PAUL REACTS —

AS LIGHTBULB IN CELL BURNS BRIGHTER.

3

PAUL POV

BULB GROWS BRIGHTER.

THE GREEN MILE

SC. 81

①

PUSH IN

①A

LIGHTBULB GETS HOTTER
AND HOTTER ...

②

ANGLE OVER BULB:

PAUL AND COFFEY

PUSH IN ON PAUL

③

③A

THE GREEN MILE

SC. 81

① LIGHTBULB EXPLODES!

② PAUL POV OF EXPLODING BULB (SAME AS PAGE 3, PANEL 2)

③ LIGHT FLASHES BRILLIANTLY ON PAUL'S FACE...

④ COFFEY RELEASES PAUL

④A PAUL COLLAPSES TO KNEES

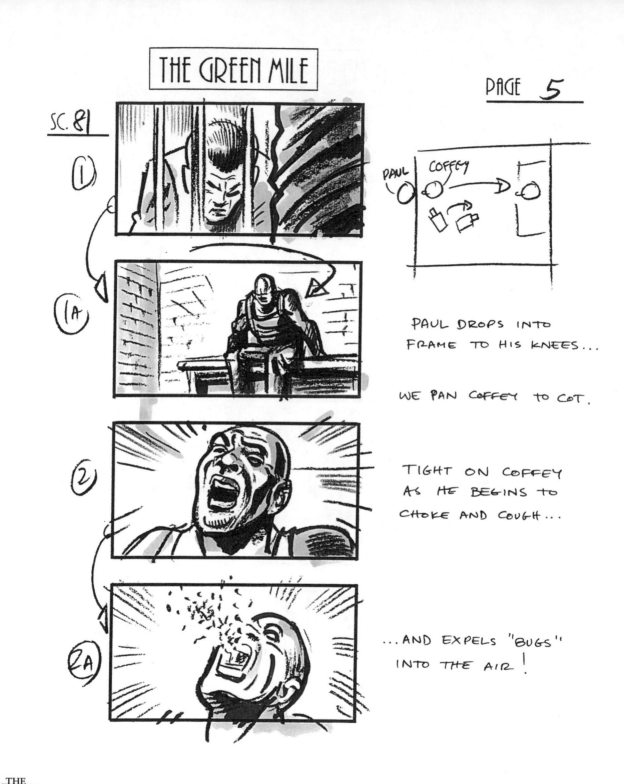

THE GREEN MILE

SC. 81

PAUL DROPS INTO
FRAME TO HIS KNEES...

WE PAN COFFEY TO COT.

TIGHT ON COFFEY
AS HE BEGINS TO
CHOKE AND COUGH...

...AND EXPELS "BUGS"
INTO THE AIR!

THE GREEN MILE

SC. 81

PUSH IN E.C.U. ON
PAUL AS HE REACTS,
GAZING UP AT THE
SWIRLING CLOUD...

HIGH ANGLE OF CELL
LOOKING DOWN AT
BOTH FIGURES...

...AS "BUGS" SWIRL
AND DISSIPATE.

END OF SEQUENCE

CAST AND CREW CREDITS

Castle Rock Entertainment
presents
A Darkwoods Production
THE GREEN MILE

Paul Edgecomb	Tom Hanks
Brutus "Brutal" Howell	David Morse
Jan Edgecomb	Bonnie Hunt
John Coffey	Michael Clarke Duncan
Warden Hal Moores	James Cromwell
Eduard Delacroix	Michael Jeter
Arlen Bitterbuck	Graham Greene
Percy Wetmore	Doug Hutchison
"Wild Bill" Wharton	Sam Rockwell
Dean Stanton	Barry Pepper
Harry Terwilliger	Jeffrey DeMunn
Melinda Moores	Patricia Clarkson
Toot-Toot	Harry Dean Stanton
Old Paul Edgecomb	Dabbs Greer
Elaine Connelly	Eve Brent
Klaus Detterick	William Sadler
Orderly Hector	Mack C. Miles
Man in Nursing Home	Rai Tasco
Lady in Nursing Home	Edrie Warner
Marjorie Detterick	Paula Malcomson
Howie Detterick	Christopher Ives
Kathe Detterick	Evanne Drucker
Cora Detterick	Bailey Drucker
Sheriff McGee	Brian Libby
Bill Dodge	Brent Briscoe
Jack Van Hay	Bill McKinney
Burt Hammersmith	Gary Sinise
Cynthia Hammersmith	Rachel Singer
Hammersmith's Son	Scotty Leavenworth
Hammersmith's Daughter	Katelyn Leavenworth

Earl the Plumber	Bill Gratton
Woman at Del's Execution	Dee Croxton
Wife at Del's Execution	Rebecca Klingler
Husband at Del's Execution	Gary Imhoff
Police Officer	Van Epperson
Reverend at Funeral	Reverend David E. Browning
Mr. Jingles	Boone's Animals for Hollywood

Stunts

Clay Boss	Danielle Burgio
H. D. Burton	Steve Chambers
Tim Davison	Tom Huff
Ray Lykins	Kerry Rossall
Clark Tucker	

Written for the Screen and Directed by	Frank Darabont
Produced by	David Valdes and
	Frank Darabont
Based on the Novel by	Stephen King
Director of Photography	David Tattersall, B.S.C.
Production Designed by	Terence Marsh
Edited by	Richard Francis-Bruce, A.C.E.
Music by	Thomas Newman
Costume Designer	Karyn Wagner
Casting by	Mali Finn, C.S.A.
Production Manager	L. Dean Jones, Jr.
First Assistant Director	Alan B. Curtiss
Second Assistant Director	David Bernstein
Second Assistant Director	Jonathan Watson
Visual Effects Supervisor	Charles Gibson
Supervising Art Director	William Cruse
Set Decorator	Michael Seirton
Stunt Coordinator—Animals	Boone Narr
Animal Trainers	Betty Linn
	Carrie Simpson
Steadicam/Camera Operator	David Emmerichs
First Assistant Camera	Heather Page
Second Assistant Camera	Jon S. Yirak
	Charles Katz
Camera Loader	Anna Castellani
Script Supervisor	Susan Malerstein-Watkins
Video Assist	Scott Crabbe
2nd Second Assistant Director	Basti van der Woude
DGA Trainee	Jodie Thomas
Dialect Coach	Jessica Drake
Assembly Editor	Alan Edward Bell

First Assistant Film Editor	Robert Charles Lusted
AVID Assistant Film Editor	Jennifer Mangan
Assistant Film Editors	Tracy Hall
	Jim Schermerhorn
	James Schulte
	Andrew Dickler
Apprentice Film Editors	Toby Francis-Bruce
	David C. Horton, Jr.
Property Master	Maureen Farley
Assistant Props	Kim Larsen
	Merdyce McClaran
Key Grip	Casey P. Jones
Best Boy Grip	Donald J. Vos
Dolly Grip	Chuck Wayt
Key Rigging Grip	Glen Purdy
Grips	Pete McAdams
	Pete Wagner
	David K. Howard
	Claude Fullerton
Gaffer	Bobby Burton
Best Boy Electric	Wayne Marshall
Rigging Gaffer	Jimmy Keys
Electricians	Justin M. Holdsworth
	Mike Sweeney
	Paul Hazard
	Larry J. Liddell
	James Peter Sobiegraj
	James K. McComas
Sound Mixer	Willie D. Burton, CAS
Boom	Marvin E. Lewis
Cableman	Robert W. Harris
Key Makeup Artist	Lois Burwell
Makeup Artist	Deborah LaMia Denauer
Key Hairstylist	Nina Paskowitz
Hairstylist	Janis Clark
Makeup Artist for Tom Hanks	Daniel Striepeke
Costume Supervisor	Paula Kaatz
Key Costumer	Heather Pain
Costumer	Lis Bothwell
Costumer to Tom Hanks	Marsha L. Bozeman
Art Department Coordinator	Beatriz Kerti
Set Designers	Donald Woodruff
	Dianne Wager
Storyboard Artist	Peter Von Sholly
Leadman	Christopher Neely
Set Dressers	Kurt T.V. VerBaarschott
	Billy Baker
	Melanie S. Chretin
	Chris F. Fielding
On Set Dresser	Jack Evans

Art Department Buyer	James Gregory Evans
Special Makeup Effects by	K.N.B. EFX Group, Inc.
Supervisors	Greg Nicotero
	Howard Berger
Sculptors	Garrett Immel
	Mark Maitre
	Gino Crognale
Lab Techs	Brian Rae
	James Hall
	H. Al Lorenzana
	Justin Ditter
	Steve Hartman
	Ron Pipes II
Office Manager	Kamar Bitar
Coordinator	Chiz Hasegawa
Puppeteers	Hiroshi Ikeuchi
	Marc Irvin
	Luke Khanlian
	Louis Kiss
	Scott Patton
Stunt Coordinator	Jeff Imada
Special Effects Coordinator	Darrell D. Pritchett
Special Effects	Corey Pritchett
Production Coordinator	Carrie DuRose
Assistant Production Coordinator	Ellen Dunn
Production Secretary	Robert L. Catron
Production Accountant	K. Lenna Katich
Post Production Accountant	Anne Scott
Assistant Production Accountants	Kelley L. Baker
	E. Gloria Alvarado
	John Semedik
Payroll Supervisor	Deborah Cornett-Anderson
Accounting Assistant	Jessica E. Klein
Still Photographer	Ralph Nelson, SMPSP
Unit Publicist	Ernie Malik
Acting Coach	Larry Moss
Casting Associates	Emily Schweber
	Maureen Whalen
Extras Casting	Charlie Messenger
Assistant to Frank Darabont	David Johnson
Assistant to David Valdes	Rossie Grose McFadden
Assistant to Tom Hanks	Amy McKenzie
Production Assistants to Frank Darabont	Brett Z. Hill
	Anna Garduño
Construction Coordinator	Sebastian Milito
Construction Foremen	Dix Stillman
	Scott Mizgaites
Construction Buyer	Edward F. LaLone
Standby Painter	Andrew R. Flores
Standby Carpenter	Eric Joseph Karas

Construction

Thomas Benardello	Dan Gilmore
Dave Howland	Sasha Madzar
Mark McGraudy	Steve Perea
Isidoro Roponi	
Transportation Coordinator	Welch Lambeth
Transportation Captains	Andy R. Straub
	Jeff Couch

Production Drivers

JB Bartlett	Ronald Wm. Cowan
David Garris	Ben C. Giller
David Haldeman	Jim Johnson
Jack C. Kilgore	Randy Lovelady
Michael Ralph Price	Lowell Smith

Set Production Assistants	Jasa Murphy
	Kevin McNamara
Office Production Assistants	Lorraine Clarkson Sachiko
	Ashley M. Armitage
Art Department P.A.	Rocco J. Hindman
Construction P.A.	Iacopo Wachter
Video Archivist	Constantine Nasr
Security	Peter Weireter
Los Angeles Catering	Home on the Range
Location Catering	TomKats Catering
Craft Services	Craig Glaser
	Cajun

Post Production Supervisor	Christy Dimmig
Sound Editorial Services provided by	Weddington Productions
Supervising Sound Editor	Mark Mangini
Supervising ADR and Dialogue Editor	Julia Evershade
Re-Recording Mixers	Robert J. Litt
	Elliot Tyson
	Michael Herbick
Sound Design	Eric Lindeman
Special Sound FX by	John P.
	Ken Johnson
Sound Editors	Howell Gibbons
	Dave Stone, MPSE
Foley Supervisor	Aaron Glascock
Foley Editor	Solange Schwalbe
Editorial Assistant	Smith Timsawat
Assistant Sound Editors	Sonny Pettijohn
	Nancy Barker
Recordists	Marsha Sorce
	Kevin Webb
ADR Mixer	Thomas J. O'Connell
ADR Recordist	Rick Canelli

Foley Mixer	Mary Jo Lang
Foley Artists	John B. Roesch
	Hilda Hodges
Foley Recordist	Carolyn Tapp
ADR Voice Casting	Barbara Harris
Music Editor	Bill Bernstein
Assistant Music Editor	Jordan Corngold
Orchestrator	Thomas Pasatieri
Music Scoring Mixer	Dennis Sands
Music Scoring Recordists	David Marquette
	Tom Hardisty
Music Contractor	Leslie Morris
Music Preparation	Julian Bratolyubov
Music Consultant	Arlene Fishbach
Titles and Opticals	Buena Vista Imaging
Color Timer	David Orr
Negative Cutter	Mo Henry

Second Unit

2nd Unit Director	Charles Gibson
Director of Photography	Mark Vargo
First Assistant Director	Liz Ryan
First Assistant Camera	Liam Clark
Second Assistant Camera	Meera Laube
Script Supervisor	Connie Papineau
Gaffer	Cory Geryak
Best Boy Electric	Jimmy Crawford
Electrican	Paul Cheung
Key Grip	Jason Newton
Dolly Grip	Brian D. Mills

Tennessee Crew

Location Manager	Mark Ragland
Asst. Production Coordinators	M. Gaye Melvin
	Krista Jacobsen Hoey
"B" Camera Operator	Robert LaBonge
"B" First Assistant Camera	Todd McMullen
"B" Second Assistant Camera	S. Beth Horton
Extras Casting	Kim Petrosky
Craft Service	Diane Johnson
Set Production Assistants	Chris Stringfield
	Carlton B. Adkins
	Jon William McWright
	Carrie Freedle
Construction	John Barbera
	Mike Minor
	John Rabasca
	Michael Adams
	Brandon Tarpy
	Sheila Bartlett

Transportation Captain	Dave Hodgin, Jr.
Mule Wrangler	Malcolm L. Jessup

Present-Day Sequences

Director of Photography	Gabriel Beristain, B.S.C.
First Assistant Director	L. Dean Jones, Jr.
Second Assistant Director	Sean Hobin
2nd Second Assistant Director	Jules Kovisars
Camera Operator	Randy Nolen
First Assistant Camera	Alan Cohen
Second Assistant Camera	Mark Brown
Camera Assistant/Loader	Anne Gentling
Location Manager	Edwin Dennis
Script Supervisor	Dea Cantu
Sound Mixer	Richard Goodman
Boom	Randy Johnson
Cableman	Todd Bassman
Key Grip	Les Percy
Best Boy Grip	Willie Mann
Dolly Grip	Michael Price
Gaffer	Mark Vuille
Best Boy Electric	Michael K. O'Melia
Key Makeup Artist	John Elliott
Key Hairstylist	Katherine Rees
Costume Supervisor	Gilda Texter
Set Decorator	Natali Pope
Leadman	Mark Woods
Art Department Assistant	Summer Valdes
Production Coordinator—North Carolina	Joanne Porzio
Assistant Production Coordinator	Victoria Person
Production Secretary	Melissa Savage
Production Assistant	Michael Peterson

Visual Effects

INDUSTRIAL LIGHT & MAGIC
A Division of Lucas Digital Ltd.
Marin County, CA

Visual Effects Supervisor	Ellen Poon
Visual Effects Producers	Stephanie Hornish
CG Supervisors	Carl Frederick
	Tom Rosseter
Digital Artists	Pat Conran
	Jiri Jacknowitz
	Jodie Maier
	Khatsho Orfali
	Bob Powell
	David Weitzberg
Film and Editorial	Kenneth Smith
Visual Effect Production	Donald Valentin

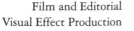

POP Film and Animation

Visual Effects Supervisor	David Sosalla
Executive Producer	Joe Gareri
Digital Effects Associate Producer	Tom Clary
Digital Effects Compositors	Michael Degtjarewsky
	Lawrence Littleton
	Tom Lamb

Rhythm and Hues

Visual Effects Producer	Chad Merriam
Animation Director	Bill Kroyer
Lighting Director	Eileen Jensen
2D Supervisor	Betsy Paterson
Animators	Brian Dowrick
	Nancy Kato
Lighting Artist	John Dietz

3d Matte Paintings by Matte World Digital

Visual Effects Supervisor	Craig Barron
Visual Effects Producer	Krystyna Demkowicz
Chief Digital Matte Artist	Chris Evans
Digital Matte Artist	Brett Northcutt
Digital Composite Supervisor	Paul Rivera
Digital Compositor	Todd R. Smith
Digital Compositor/Animation	Mike Root

"CHARMAINE"
Written by Lew Pollack and Erno Rapee
Performed by Montovani
Courtesy of LaserLight Digital and San Juan Music Group
by arrangement with Source/Q

"OLD ALABAMA"
Written and recorded by Alan Lomax
Performed by B.B. And Group
Courtesy of Rounder Records
by arrangement with Ocean Park Music Group

"STARDUST"
Written by Mitchell Parish and Hoagy Carmichael
Performed by Eddy Howard
Courtesy of Columbia Records
by arrangement with Sony Music Licensing

"THREE LITTLE WORDS"
Written by Bert Kaimar and Harry Ruby
Performed by Duke Ellington
Courtesy of The RCA Records Label of BMG Entertainment

"WRAP YOUR TROUBLES IN DREAMS
(AND DREAM YOUR TROUBLES AWAY)"
Written by Ted Koehler, Billy Moll, and Harry Barris
Performed by Eddy Howard
Courtesy of Columbia Records
by arrangement with Sony Music Licensing

"CHEEK TO CHEEK"
Written by Irving Berlin
Performed by Fred Astaire
Courtesy of Turner Entertainment Co.

"OLD FASHIONED LOVE"
Written by Jamers P. Johnson and Cecil Mack
Performed by Eddy Howard
Courtesy of Columbia Records
by arrangement with Sony Music Licensing

"I CAN'T GIVE YOU ANYTHING BUT LOVE"
Written by Jimmy McHugh and Dorothy Fields
Performed by Billie Holiday
Courtesy of Columbia Records
by arrangement with Sony Music Licensing

"DID YOU EVER SEE A DREAM WALKING"
Written by Harry Revel and Mack Gordon
Performed by Gene Austin
Courtesy of Columbia Records
by arrangement with Sony Music Licensing

"CHARMAINE"
Performed by Guy Lombardo and His Royal Canadians
Courtesy of Columbia Records
by arrangement with Sony Music Licensing

The appearance of Mr. Fred Astaire has been arranged through
a special license with Mrs. Fred Astaire, Beverly Hills, California.
All rights reserved.

"Top Hat" courtesy of Turner Entertainment Co.

"JERRY SPRINGER" ® Show excerpts from
Studios USA Television Distribution, LLC

Filmed with PANAVISION Cameras & Lenses

Camera Cranes & Dollies provided by
Chapman/Leonard Studio Equipment, Inc.
J. L. Fisher, Inc.

Re-Recorded at Warner Hollywood Studios

Music Recorded at
Todd AO Scoring Stage
Signet Soundelux

Color and Prints by
Technicolor ®

KODAK
Motion Picture Products

The Producers wish to gratefully thank:
The People of the State of Tennessee and Governor Don Sundquist
The Tennessee Film, Entertainment and Music Commission
The Tennessee Department of Corrections
The North Carolina State Film Office

Special thanks to:
Stephen King

American Humane Association monitored the treatment of all animals.
No animals were harmed in the making of this motion picture.

Filmed at the Warner Hollywood Studios, West Hollywood, California,
and on location in Nashville, Tennessee, and Blowing Rock, North Carolina.

The characters and incidents portrayed and the names used herein are fictitious,
and any similarity to any name or incident, or the character or biography of any person,
is purely coincidental and unintentional.

This motion picture photoplay is protected pursuant to the provisions of the laws
of the United States of America and other countries. Unauthorized duplication,
distribution or exhibition of this photoplay may result in criminal prosecution.

This motion picture is being exhibited under specific license and is not for sale.
Castle Rock Entertainment is the author of this motion picture for the purpose
of copyright and other laws.

Copyright © 1999 CR Films, LLC
All Rights Reserved.

RELEASED BY WARNER BROS.

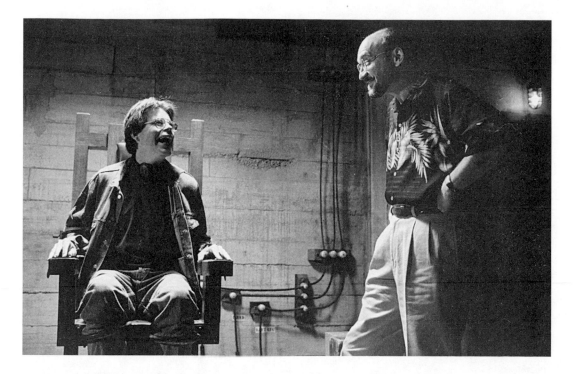

STEPHEN EDWIN KING was born in 1947 in Portland, Maine, the second son of Donald and Nellie Ruth Pillsbury King. He attended the University of Maine at Orono, where he secured a B.S. in English that qualified him to teach at the high school level. He and Tabitha Spruce met as students, and were married in 1971. That same year, Stephen began teaching classes at a public high school in Hampden, Maine. His stunning writing career took off in 1973 with the publication of his first novel, *Carrie,* the success of which allowed him to leave teaching and pursue writing full-time. He has since become the best-selling author of all time with books such as *The Shining, Salem's Lot, The Stand, The Dead Zone,* and many subsequent works too numerous to mention here. His serialized novel, *The Green Mile,* climbed to the top of the best-seller lists in 1996, and became the basis for the 1999 Castle Rock Entertainment film. Stephen and Tabitha King live in Bangor, Maine, and have three children: Naomi Rachel, Joe Hill, and Owen Phillip.

FRANK ARPAD DARABONT was born in 1959 in Montbéliard, France, the son of Hungarian refugees who had fled Budapest during the failed 1956 revolution. Brought to America as an infant, Frank graduated from Hollywood High School in 1977 and began his film career as a production assistant on a low-budget 1980 horror movie entitled *Hell Night.* He spent the next six years in set dressing and set construction while struggling to break through as a screenwriter. In 1986, people started paying Frank to write, which he's been gratefully doing ever since. His first feature film as a director was 1994's *The Shawshank Redemption,* adapted from the novella by Stephen King. *Shawshank* was nominated for seven Academy Awards, including Best Picture and Best Adapted Screenplay, and Frank was nominated as Best Director by the Directors Guild of America. Frank is very happy to be continuing his association with Mr. King on his follow-up film to *Shawshank,* an adaptation of King's acclaimed serial novel, *The Green Mile.*